LAU

Martha,
May all your adventures
be harmonious!

NEWCOMER

The St. Cross Choir Series

Book 1

outskirts
press

Newcomer
The St. Cross Choir Series, Book 1

v3.0

Outskirts Press, Inc.
http://www.outskirtspress.com

ISBN: 978-1-4787-8529-3

PRINTED IN THE UNITED STATES OF AMERICA

For Lisa

Note: No dogs were injured in the writing of this novel.

1

Frank O'Brien chewed on an idea as he walked the scrappy dog along a woodland trail near the animal shelter. He didn't like where his thoughts were leading.

The facility manager rounded the corner to the shelter entrance to find an unattended cat carrier standing by the front door. The sight pushed the ruminations out of his mind. The occupant, by the sound of it, was not happy.

So much for my dinner, Frank mused, knowing that the time until choir practice would be eaten up by intake procedures.

Gently lifting the carrier, he walked the stray husky to its kennel. Next, he headed to the cat room. Buck Lee, a longtime staff member, looked up from refilling the water bowls. "Shouldn't you be outta here by now?" Buck asked.

Frank, whose face was weathered and tan from years spent outdoors, shook his head. “Must be some kind of curse,” he said. “Always seems to happen when I have a rehearsal.”

“Then quit the choir, man. We’re full up. There’s no more room at the inn.”

With a grunt, Frank turned his attention to the animal in the carrier and put on gauntlet-style gloves. The extended cuffs would protect his hands and forearms if the transfer to a cage upset the gray cat. His efforts were met with mewling, but the feline submitted to being handled. Mission accomplished, he pulled off the gloves, sat on a small stool, and started filling in the cage-tag information. When Frank was about halfway finished, he glanced up to see Buck staring at him.

“What’s bugging you?” Buck asked. The younger man had his straight hair pulled back in a long ponytail that rested along his spine. A few gray strands stood out against the jet black. “I’ve worked with you enough years to know when something’s not right.”

“That transparent, huh?” Frank asked. He let the silence stretch out like a highway to the horizon and continued with his task.

Frank had begun to piece together a disturbing pattern. Small acts of vandalism – that bore the appearance of minor accidents – were taking place with increasing frequency at the Northern

California church where he sang in the choir and served on the board of directors.

So far, no one had been hurt. No real damage had occurred. But the events were troublesome nonetheless. They were out of order. Something was amiss, and it seemed to center on the St. Cross Church choir, which had recently been joined by singers from the local choral society to perform the Duruflé Requiem.

"I might as well talk to the cats," Buck said. He returned to measuring food into the small bowls lined up along the narrow shelf.

Frank grunted and resumed his thoughts.

The first hint of any irregularity had occurred several weeks earlier on the initial Thursday night rehearsal of the combined groups. Frank was early for choir practice and anticipated a short wait in the brisk evening air before the music director showed up to unlock the church. But the choir room door swung open when Frank grasped the ornate knob.

At the time, he chalked the anomaly up to the custodian – or perhaps forgetfulness on the organist's part. She often practiced on the aging pipe organ in the afternoons. That the heavy wooden door stood closed but unlocked was nothing other than a security risk.

But two weeks earlier, Frank arrived at rehearsal shortly after the director to find him picking up hymnals off the floor. Adam Frasier seemed distracted by the mess but offered no explanation.

Then last week, Frank entered the practice room to find a hand bell case had fallen off a back shelf and somehow opened. Several of the high-treble bells were lying on a table and the worn wooden floor. Once again, Adam was tidying up the disarray.

Frank had suspicions that something unorthodox was occurring.

Buck cleared his throat and tried again. "Maybe," he said, "you need a vacation."

Frank shrugged as if to throw off the suggestion. The tiny no-kill shelter was filled to capacity. A vacation wasn't going to change that.

Unscrupulous folks were known to dump dogs in the wilderness of the 400-mile-long Sierra Nevada mountain range. Family pets became separated from their hiking or hunting partners. The unfortunate canines sometimes formed unruly packs, but many wandered alone until they were taken down by wolves or bears. Others starved while waiting by the side of the road, or they succumbed to the elements.

Nearly a third of the shelter's animals showed up during off-hours and were left anonymously on site. Once, a dog with a broken leg was found tethered in the parking lot. The more Frank worked with animals, the less he liked people.

The male cat that Frank was attending

seemed physically unharmed from whatever journey had brought the tom to the concrete-block and chain-link enclosure. Fortunately, the animal had landed well. Although surrounded by a wilderness of sheer granite mountains and dense pine forests, the tranquil town of St. Cross was home to a well-financed animal facility, set up by one of the town's benefactors.

"Maybe you need a woman."

Buck's comment brought a small smile to Frank's face. "Don't I always." He finished the paperwork, slid the document into a plastic sleeve, and attached it to the newcomer's cage.

"No, I'm good," Frank said. "Just hope I'm not too ripe-smelling for the other tenors in my section tonight. This has been one long, dirty day."

Buck gave him a sideways glance.

"Always chill to talk to you, Frank," he said. Then the two men headed in opposite directions.

Recent St. Cross arrival Harper Henshaw wanted to scream into the forest. But who was there to hear the single woman on a wooded acre at the outskirts of town?

A ring on her cell arrived like a lifeboat pulling alongside a sinking ship. She recognized the caller ID and pressed TALK.

"Gene," Harper said to her former editor, "I'm so glad to hear from you. Your timing couldn't be better. I was ready to hear a friendly voice."

"How could it not be?" he asked. "Let's review: You left your reporting job and longtime friends, took care of your folks and then never returned. I really thought you'd be back. No part of that took into consideration how much you'd miss me."

"True," she said. "You were the perfect 'work husband.' I don't miss the newspaper though, just a few of the people there, like you."

"Too bad," he said. "We'll always have an opening here for you. But I was hoping you'd consider freelancing for me. There are a lot of potential environmental stories up there, and I've got no reporters to send."

"I never said I don't miss the work. In fact, I could use the income. My 'affordable dream house' up here is rapidly becoming a nightmare. The problems are piling up – roof rot, plumbing woes, cracks in the foundation. I didn't expect my nest egg to be devoured so quickly. What was I thinking?"

Harper looked about and took in her somewhat dingy 1920s bungalow. Every room needed fresh paint. The kitchen was impractical in its current state. The top two cabinet shelves were beyond the reach of the short redhead.

"I take it that's a rhetorical question," Gene said. "How are you doing, really?"

Harper took a deep breath before plunging ahead.

"Not great. I've tried to plug into community activities, but this place is no newsroom. Lively conversations among well-informed, strong-headed people? So far, they're hard to come by. And I guess I hadn't realized what an adrenaline junkie I am. I find myself getting bored without the pressure of daily deadlines."

"Humph," Gene muttered into the phone. She could hear him clicking at his keyboard and waited patiently. "Sorry. I had to answer that right away."

"I understand." She remained silent while Gene typed a reply to the almost instantaneous response he had received.

"Now," he said. "Where were we? Any love life up there?"

"In that respect, this place is just like the newsroom – a dating desert."

"Then you should feel right at home," Gene said. He was never above a good jab. "But how are you doing, really?"

"Well look at the old reporter in you," Harper said. "Going back in again to flesh out the details." She dropped the joking for a bit to give him a straight answer.

Harper sighed. "Fighting depression.

Questioning why I picked such a remote and small town. A fresh start seemed just like what I needed, but cutting ties to longtime friends and familiar places? Now I'm not sure I can replace all that in mid-life.

"I think the only thing that's keeping me sane is singing in the church choir." There her solid soprano voice blended with others into a single organism – a whole larger than the sum of its parts. The sounds echoing through the drafty old church drowned out her nagging self-doubt and made her feel as though perhaps she *could* belong in St. Cross.

Gene's voice brought her back to the moment.

"I'm sorry it's been so tough, Harper," he said. "You know I'm here for you."

"Thanks, Gene."

"Now about those freelance stories – pitch them as you find them. We're particularly interested in what's happening in the forests this year with the extended drought and bark beetle infestation. Did you see the latest UCLA report saying that the state drought might last indefinitely?"

"Yeah, I read that. I can tell you already that this part of the range is nothing like what I remember from childhood vacations. Large swaths of pines are standing dead and brown."

"That's a great place to start. Find a couple of vantage points and shoot the same scene once a month. If the landscape is changing as rapidly as I suspect it is, we'll have some telling photo galleries before long. Also I'll send you some reports on the firefighter shortage. Depending on how the fire season develops this year, that could be a real concern. I've got another call coming in. Gotta go."

"No worries. Thanks again, Gene. Catch you later."

At the sound of the dial tone, Harper's thoughts returned to choir practice. She had heard something last week about a bell case sliding off a shelf. One hand bell had gone astray – an F, in fact. *Who would take one hand bell,* she wondered.

"Who indeed?" she asked, but only the wind in the trees, the chatter of chipmunks, and the ticking of her kitchen clock replied.

In his cabin home at the foot of a mountain, P.W. Simpson held a stark white envelope in his wrinkled hands. He had a proverb stuck in his head. The senior citizen couldn't remember if the saying was Biblical or not. *All good things must come to an end.*

If pressed, he leaned toward it being a piece of poetry.

P.W., as Phinehas Walters Simpson was

known, had forgotten so much more than he retained these days that the church caretaker often just tried to rely on the sense of things. Why would all good things come to an end?

Now, Edith. He fingered the notice from the law firm that represented the estate of his long-dead friend Edith Saint Cross. *I think I've had about enough of this.*

He rose slowly from his seat at the dining room table and went into the bedroom. There he placed the envelope in a dresser drawer, on top of a packet of similar-looking correspondence.

At a pounding on his front door, P.W. navigated his way back through the living room to the entryway. He opened the door without bothering to check the peephole. His friend Frank stood on the front stoop. In Frank's right hand was another formal letter on high-quality paper stock from the partnership of Grayson & Sleigh.

"What's going on?" Frank asked, as though P.W. could read Edith's mind two decades beyond the grave.

"Nice to see you too, Frank. Come on in, and I'll get us some coffee."

Frank entered, but shook his head from side to side. "No. I'll make the coffee. Yours could eat through the hull of a battleship."

"No!" P.W. was emphatic. "That's the way I like it. Anyway, the pot is still nearly full. Just reheat what's there. You can call it espresso, or add some water to yours."

Frank sighed his assent and headed to the kitchen. As he moved around the familiar room, Frank pondered the formal letter. His life had taken an unexpected turn 10 years earlier when he had found himself on the receiving end of Edith's generosity. A codicil to her will had resulted in his heading the animal shelter. Although the financial analyst had little intention of changing careers at the time, the enticement was such that he couldn't in good conscience say no. Edith had her ways of getting what she wanted. Should he accept the position, funds would be transferred to the public library for a new roof. Peer pressure would have gotten him, even if he had tried to wiggle out from beneath Edith's thumb.

Plus, Frank had been ready for a change. Without his wife Teresa at his side, building toward a mutual future, he had felt adrift in his life and career. Sometimes he wondered whether Edith had been prescient.

Frank rattled about the kitchen, putting things away, wiping down the counters, and scouring the sink while the coffee reheated. Then he filled two mugs, put milk in both, and joined P.W. at the dining room table. Pushing the sugar bowl toward the older man, he sat and sipped his coffee.

P.W. spoke when he finally finished stirring. "So I called over there and spoke with that nice Patricia Grayson. Seems old Edith has another codicil that involves us. No doubt she's gonna shake things up."

"Us?" Frank asked. "Just the two of us?"

"Nope. Seems there's a third to our little party." P.W. reached into the pocket of his flannel shirt and withdrew a scrap of paper on which he had scrawled a name and phone number.

Frank deciphered the shaky lettering as "Harper Henshaw," but the name meant nothing to him. "Who's this?"

"That's the redhead just joined the choir," P.W. said. "Apparently the lawyers sent a letter to her, too, as the newest landowner in St. Cross."

Frank shook his head in confusion. "Okay. I'll call this Harper and see if she wants to carpool to the law office in Alta next week. Maybe we can learn something on the way." He took another swig of his coffee and rose. "Isn't that just like Edith to throw in a wild card?"

P.W. didn't answer. He had left the present to focus on a point in the past when he and Edith were young. Frank would get no more information out of him.

2

St. Cross Choir practice always started with snacks.

"This is not supposed to be a meal, you know," organist Mimi Okada Frasier admonished a pair of tenors navigating their way back to their seats with paper plates piled high.

Rehearsals had built-in time at the beginning for fellowship and announcements. The requirement was part of the long set of instructions left by the wealthy Cross family, which had established the church and left the institution funded in perpetuity. A board ruled the church's day-to-day operations. A pastor shared with another church and the occasional pulpit-fill minister took care of sermon duties on Sunday mornings.

The accompanist and her husband Adam,

who directed the choir, had supplied the treats tonight as the assembled kicked off their first full-voice rehearsal of the Duruflé Requiem chorus. Although not normally mean-spirited, Mimi had underestimated the number of hungry students from Sierra Foothills College who would turn out to participate with the combined forces of the existing church choir and the St. Cross Choral Society.

Adam would be hearing from some of the longtime church members if the food didn't hold out. Many of the regular singers were retirement age or elderly. They valued the social time as a break from their somewhat isolated lives in the mountain community.

Mimi snatched a grape on her way to the rehearsal piano, enjoying the feel of the smooth globe in her fingers.

"All right, people, time to get to work," Adam said. His booming bass voice commanded immediate attention. He always timed his rehearsal downbeat for precisely 7:20 p.m.

"There are nine movements, although some will be handled ably by mezzo-soprano and baritone soloists. Mimi, who is serving as our rehearsal pianist, will be our concert organist, and I'm hoping the church board will sign off on our hiring an orchestra. That's why there are so many of you. A special welcome to our college singers who traveled some 20 miles to 'swell' our ranks – to use a little organ humor. I'm sure their 'pipes' will enhance our sound, and we'll get through the work without too many 'stops.' Now for my students, I suggest you familiarize yourselves with the organ terms swell, pipes and stops before tomorrow's pop quiz." Several groans rose from the college crowd.

High schooler Samantha Hernandez jerked her head up and looked at the conductor as though he had lost his mind. "What is this, 'Jeopardy'?" she said under her breath. "I'll take parts of the pipe organ for $500, Alex."

The slouching teenager was both peeved and embarrassed to be at the rehearsal. She hadn't sung in a choir or been in a church since grade school, and she was doing so under duress.

Sammie, as she was known, had been caught with "inappropriate material" on her smart phone. So her parents were in the process of making her life miserable. She was being forced to volunteer at the animal shelter and was required to do some other sort of service work, as well. Singing a Requiem for seven weeks had seemed preferable to taking meals to old people rotting in their shabby homes.

"Better to sing about death," she had told her mom, "than watch it happen."

What she hadn't counted on was the influx of the college crowd at this, the fourth rehearsal, to "swell the ranks" as the director had proclaimed. Things could start to get interesting. Sammie might be able to pass for a college freshman. She'd lay low this week, head buried in the score. Next week, though, it was game on: makeup, freshly washed hair, and casual yet stylish clothes.

Being part of a choir might be new to Sammie, but for Harper, it was wonderfully familiar. She found the experience a source of peace and comfort, at least when she was actually singing. From her involvement in a lifetime of choirs, however, she knew every group had its minor irritations. This appeared to be true in St. Cross too.

Several singers were unhappy with the director's selection of Maurice Duruflé's mass for the dead for the upcoming concert.

"Didn't we perform this Requiem three years ago?" Harper overheard one ancient bass grumble.

And why sing what was essentially a Roman Catholic prayer for souls relegated to Purgatory in a nondenominational but decidedly Protestant church, another singer had complained. If people were faithful and going to heaven, God certainly knew. How could praying for the process to speed up make any difference?

One elderly tenor randomly spoke out against the doxology that was sung every week during worship. "It goes against natural body rhythms."

In addition to theological and musical divisions, ability and application were coming into play during rehearsals. Some of the regular singers were struggling with their notes and holding back the group's progress on the Requiem, a much harder work than the normal Sunday fare. For the most part, singers from the St. Cross Choral Society were either far better musicians or had done more preparation work than the church members.

More than one alto was prone to snide comments about the sopranos, who were having trouble staying on pitch. For their part, the altos had too much vibrato to effectively produce a unified choral sound.

Apparently the Choral Society soprano directly in front of Harper found her singing either too loud or off pitch. The woman occasionally turned back to glare at her.

"Roll the *R*s!"

Adam's voice jolted Harper from her thoughts.

"Feel the underlying pulse independently of the accompaniment," he said. "Give the notes energy when you move to another pitch, and articulate each of the changed notes."

The director's comments continued in sharp contrast to the introit's soothing accompaniment, which made Harper think of incense wafting in the air. "Watch the tempo eight measures after rehearsal number four," he said. "We're slowing down there.

"Choir, do you know where I am? When I say rehearsal four I mean the number in the box above the staff, not the page number. The orchestra members will have different scores with different page numbers. We all need to use the rehearsal numbers to stay on task."

"Rest eternal," "perpetual light," the lyrics proclaimed in Latin.

"Ladies, ladies!" Adam released a fist for emphasis. "Center the vibrato on the pitch so the notes just float."

Measure after measure the choir progressed with pauses for tonal agreement, rhythm corrections, and a somewhat long-winded discussion of the importance of pianissimo, piano, mezzo piano, mezzo forte, and forte volume distinctions.

"The work is not so terribly challenging, but has its aspects," Adam said at the conclusion of the evening's practice. "The one thing we can't do in this is to get behind. See you next week."

Harper closed her score and was collecting her personal possessions when a fit middle-aged man approached her. The graying hair at his temples caused her to wonder if his physique made him look younger than he was.

"Hi, I'm Frank O'Brien. I called about carpooling into Alta on Thursday. I'm not sure how we got this many weeks into rehearsal without me having introduced myself."

"Harper Henshaw," she said, shaking his extended hand. "I suspect there are lots of new faces."

"Not so many as you'd think." He seemed distracted by the sight of a teenager making her way down from the alto section. Harper turned to notice the young woman also was catching the eye of one of the college basses.

"I'm sorry," Frank said, refocusing on Harper. "I'm just surprised to see one of my teen volunteers from the animal shelter here. Next week then."

3

If Frank had thought he would learn much about Harper on the 30-minute ride to the law office, he was mistaken. She peppered him and P.W. with questions during the drive.

Frank kept his eyes on the road and let P.W. provide the bulk of the answers.

"Well, anyone who knows anything about the history of St. Cross would understand why today's meeting has put Frank on edge," P.W. said.

Frank glared at him briefly in the rear-view mirror. "I am not on edge," he said through gritted teeth.

Nonplussed, P.W. continued his narrative.

"Edith was the last in the long line of benefactors of this community, which is named St. Cross for the family. Edith and I practically grew up together, my family working for hers. She was often like an older sister, other times a co-conspirator in our many adventures, and on rare occasion she pulled rank as the boss's daughter."

P.W. explained how Edith's family had deeded land for most of the town's public areas and private institutions as each generation passed on. The church dated to her grandparents' day, the parklands to her folks, and the animal shelter to Edith herself near the end of her lifetime.

When the wealthy and eccentric spinster's will was read 20 years earlier, she had left very specific instructions in place on the running of the church, the choral society, and the animal shelter – all of which her estate continued to fund to one degree or another.

"I thought that the reading of her will would be the end of Edith's story," P.W. said, "but she apparently wasn't having any of it – even if she was dead. Not to speak ill, but Lord that woman could be a meddler – determined to see her hometown thrive with or without her. So she and the lawyers cooked up these codicils to be read at different intervals."

Every few years or so another one triggered an unexpected windfall for a fortunate institution or provided for some unmet public need.

P.W. warmed to his tale. "Then, 10 years ago, her lawyers produced the longest codicil yet.

That one upset the fruit cart. Of all things, she named me church caretaker. Just shows you her wicked sense of humor."

"How so?" Harper asked.

"I'd never been much of a churchgoer outside Easter, Christmas, and the occasional funeral, so I figured this was her idea of a little joke, just between us," P.W. said. "Well, she may have been chuckling from the great beyond, but the job was a godsend. I had unexpectedly taken on the care of my then-infant great nephew Aza. An income, benefits, and work that let me bring along a small boy prone to exploring ... well, that just fit me like a glove on the hand of God. If God wears gloves, that is."

He looked out the window and watched the scenery speed by for a moment "She was serving her interests and mine – putting someone she could trust on the staff of the family's beloved church."

That week marked almost two decades since Edith's passing. P.W. knew what his summons was about. He knew as well what Saint Edith, as he often referred to her in jest, had up the sleeve of her shroud. The sands of time, it seemed, would not be erasing her footprints anytime soon.

The remainder of the carpool ride down the mountain to the county seat of Alta was collegial. The trio used the time to become better acquainted and listened to the portion of the Requiem that had been assigned as their homework.

P.W. joked that for Edith Saint Cross, "eternal rest" didn't seem to be in the books.

The ride back up to St. Cross, however, was the polar opposite of the cheerful time spent getting to the city. What had felt like short intervals of companionable silence on the way into town felt increasingly strained. Frank was furious; P.W., pleased; Harper, stunned.

Edith had done it once again – played God with select residents of St. Cross and assigned their destinies into the future. Each had emerged with news to fume over, share, or try to keep secret.

Although his foot maintained a steady speed along the winding roads, Frank's mind was racing. He could barely contain his anger. "What is she playing at?" he said at last. "Of all the gold-arned cockamamie mixed-up power-hungry games money can buy …."

"Lord have mercy," P.W. said from the backseat of Frank's truck. "I take it you didn't receive good news, Frank. What's the matter?"

"I'm out of a job that I actually liked, and I wouldn't have even taken if Edith hadn't made me do it," he said. "And to make matters worse, I now have another job that I would never take."

Here Frank paused and studied P.W.'s time-worn face in the rear-view mirror. The man looked happy. In fact, he seemed to be beaming.

"What?" Frank yelled at P.W. "What?"

"Excuse me," Harper said, trying to bring the emotional volume down a notch. "You're saying you are out of a job, and I've been told I suddenly have one. Am I correct in recalling that you run the animal shelter?"

Frank wrenched his head toward the passenger seat and did a double-take. "Damn. You're the new head of the shelter?" Harper pursed her lips and nodded her head almost imperceptibly.

"If I so choose," she said hastily. "But I certainly wouldn't put you out of a job – just, there's this catch up. If I accept the position, then 20 acres of unused meadowland at the back of St. Cross Park will be deeded to the city for use as a dog park. If I don't ... the project is a nonstarter."

Frank slapped his hand on the steering wheel. "Puppet master," he said. "Okay, P.W. What are you so cheery about?" The elder gentleman had taken on the countenance of the Cheshire Cat.

"I've just been retired as church caretaker, complete with a pension," he said. "I guess the old girl knew I would be getting along in years and ready for a rest."

"Whoa," Frank said. "That makes my decision easier. I'm the new church caretaker if I want improvements funded for the pound. But nothing is ever simple where Edith is concerned. What gives?"

"Oh, she threw in a few bombshells," P.W. said. "First up, I'm replacing you as chairman of the church board, Frank.

"Second, parts of the budget will be taking some pretty heavy hits – particularly the music program. Lawyer said the investments that fund the church took a beating last year."

Frank, who had headed the board for several years, shook his head in disbelief. "Wow," he said. "Well, I guess we'll have to start calling you the Big W."

Harper struggled to make sense of Edith's strange will, with its sporadic codicils stretching out into time.

"Why would anyone do this?" she asked.

P.W. responded. "Well, near as I can tell she wanted to have a say in the future of St. Cross. Keep it on the right path. She was very serious about the community that bears the family name being a place that was worthwhile, where people could belong. I guess she thought a church and a choral society would be like anchors for the community. The animal shelter was her personal project. She didn't want to see the family funds mismanaged or squandered. Edith wanted her fortune to stand for something.

"The truth of the matter is, I'm not sure how well that's working out. The church has pretty sparse attendance most Sundays and wouldn't be able to survive financially without the endowment. Seems like a lot of money going to serve just a few. And if we didn't have the college students and choral society members, the small choir could never pull off the major works the estate funds."

Harper considered his answer. "I don't quite understand what the choral society is," she said. "And how it works into all this."

"The choral society is separate from the church and has only a small stipend," P.W. said. "It's supposed to have monthly use of space up at the old Cross family home, but since the most recent owner died, the property has been in probate. So, for now, the members are active only for the two major works each year at the church and in the summer, when the church choir is off.

"In the old days," he said, "there were always music salons and recitals up at the big house. That's how I first got interested in singing – by listening."

"Getting back to the codicil terms," Harper said, "they are so random. Seriously, what if I don't accept the position at the shelter? I could already be fully employed, incapable of the task, or a fugitive from the law."

Frank maneuvered past some road workers clearing a fallen tree, then fielded the question. "Oh, there's usually some back-up plan. Second newest landowner will be offered the job. That type of thing. One thing Edith never tired of was power and wielding it. Setting this up must have given her great joy.

"Although her arrangements are unusual, the lawyers put their stamp of approval on it. Nothing has ever been contested – not that there's anyone left to do the contesting."

The changing of roles was to phase in over the next several weeks. The trio fell silent as they pondered the news.

For Harper, the unexpected work would help alleviate the problem of paying for her home repairs. A one-year opt-out clause meant she could apply herself to freelance writing full-time after the bills were paid. Perhaps the experience would help her connect more quickly with other members of the community.

P.W. broke the silence. "I reckon Edith is smiling up in heaven, sitting at the right hand of God or whatever prime seat she has finagled for herself. Imagine me, a black man, the son of a Cross family servant, running the show at church."

He wouldn't have thought this possible

earlier in his lifetime, but the world had changed. The once nearly all-white St. Cross had added different shades of brown over the years, as well as foreigners and some same-sex couples. Although most of the newer residents weren't churchgoers, SCC was the only game in town. On holidays the pews were crammed.

Frank, although he remained somewhat miffed, was beginning to think the changes were perhaps in order. He was nagged lately about things seeming "off" in the church facilities on rehearsal nights. P.W. appeared oblivious to the problem. Perhaps the old guy was slowing down. By being on hand, Frank could monitor the situation.

His first order of business would be to change all the locks on the church doors as soon as he could get a locksmith out, and then he'd distribute new keys.

The threesome made it back to St. Cross in plenty of time to take care of personal business and still arrive promptly for the Thursday evening rehearsal.

Frank was on alert for anything amiss. Last week, someone had been smoking in the choir room before rehearsal. He'd picked up the scent of stale tobacco when he'd arrived, and he had found a butt in the trashcan. And the high F bell was missing.

"Now," Adam said, his booming voice signaling the end of the social time, "the Kyrie is a really hard movement for the organ and orchestra. Although there's some doubling of the instruments and voices, you're going to have to know your part independently of the accompaniment."

The assembled chorus dutifully trudged through the remaining note learning, or "wood-shedding," as the director called it. "Don't get too loud too soon. Wait until after measure 11 to start building. I know we didn't get to all the notes. You'll have to learn them for homework."

If Adam thought a rehearsal was going well or poorly, he rarely let on. His was an end game. Notes, words, rhythm, and volume had to be established before true music could result.

The choir's lone teenaged soprano, however, was chalking up the evening so far as a dismal failure. She had tried to move to the inside of her row to sit next to a college-age tenor, but matronly Judy Carey had protested.

"That is *my* seat, my dear," the bifocaled woman said. "We have a seating chart. Try to stick to it."

Sammie ducked her head and swore under her breath. She now understood why she had overheard a choir member refer to the woman as "Judy on duty." The teen shifted her weight from one hip to the next throughout the evening, anxious to be away from the odious people surrounding her.

The review of the first movement from last week went much better than the new sections. Mimi's fingers stroked the piano keys and brought forth a delicate sound that evoked ripples of water on a placid lake. The chant of the men provided a steady anchor while the women's voices gently floated above with angelic expression. "Et lux perpetua." Light eternal. After another hour, the rehearsal was over.

"See you next week, singers," Adam said, breaking the mood. "Homework, homework."

Sammie took this as her cue to sashay down to the front and try out the pick-up line she had been rehearsing all week. But within arm's reach of a group of college students, she lost her nerve.

As she turned to leave, her face starting to burn with a mixture of embarrassment and self-loathing, a voice broke through the hubbub. "Hey, aren't you in a class of mine?" asked the bass who had caught her eye last week.

"I don't think so," Sammie said. "Maybe."

"I'm Jim," he said, glancing at her name tag. "And you're Sammie? You want a ride back to school?"

“Not tonight,” Sammie said. “Ah. I’ve got to stay after and help the director.”

“Help the director what? Are you a soloist?”

Sammie tried to cover her deceit. “I mean, ah, he’s helping me with a paper – on the Requiem.”

“Cool,” Jim said. “Sec you next week.”

Sammie sighed with a mixture of pleasure, relief, and just a titch of disgust. When had she become such an easy liar?

4

Saturday morning started like any other at P.W.'s house. Aza industriously plowed through his breakfast cereal, eager to get outside with his dog Sheldon and do some hiking.

P.W., however, had instructions for him first. "I've got to run out of town today, so Uncle Frank will pick you up at 10. You can spend the day with him on his rounds at the pound and church." P.W. peered over the top of his reading glasses and saw that the boy was on the verge of protesting.

"Na-uh," P.W. said. "I am feeling every one of my close to 90 years today and in no mood for dissension. Do not dare complain, and while you're at it, use your spoon properly like a young man, not an infant. Hold it like this."

P.W. demonstrated for the blank-faced 11-year-old.

"That's complicated," Aza said. "I don't do complicated."

"Well, *do* being on time," P.W. said. "Be here by ten to 10 at the latest so you don't keep Mr. O'Brien waiting around. Now scoot."

Frank wasn't arriving any earlier because he had to pick up Harper. First they'd have breakfast, then they'd fetch Aza before heading back to the shelter to go over the weekly and long-term tasks that would need Harper's attention. She had been able to muddle through a few partial shifts already because a few key staffers knew the drill. Many days there were no pickups or intakes – only the feeding, care, and exercise of the existing "guests," as Frank called them. But today, he'd give Harper the full overview.

Is this a breakfast date? Harper wondered, examining some gray in her red hair in the bathroom mirror. *Nah. Probably more of a business meeting.*

Yet it was as close as she had come to a date during her months in St. Cross, and she took extra care getting ready.

"What outfit is appropriate for cleaning out kennels yet looks sexy?" she asked aloud.

In the days of struggle surrounding her folks' deaths and closing up the family home, she hadn't thought looking good would ever be important again. How short-sighted, she realized. There was nothing to be done this morning about the pad of flesh where her waist once had been or the crow's feet sprouting from the corners of the eyes staring back at her.

Truth be told, she did want to be able to impress a man, to hold someone's hand again and, who knows, maybe have a relationship. She found it hard to imagine a life that would never again involve sex. She was too young to throw in the towel.

First things first, she thought, shimmying into snug blue jeans and pairing them with boots, a scarf, and a cowl-neck sweater.

Before long, Frank pulled into her driveway in his truck.

"I hope you don't mind," he said as she greeted him at her front door. "We're just going to the local greasy spoon. There aren't a lot of options in a small town."

"I'm sure it will be fine," Harper said. She immediately felt overdressed when she saw Frank's well-worn work shirt. To hide her discomfort, she chattered almost nonstop as Frank drove.

The atmosphere at the Coffee Klatch Café was pleasant, and bright sunshine flooded their window table. Frank's muscular state belied the breakfast he packed away – pancakes, eggs, bacon, and a biscuit washed down with black coffee.

"Working at the shelter must be a very active job," she said, watching him consume the equivalent of her entire caloric intake for a day in one meal. She picked at a three-egg ham-and-cheese scramble with a side of fruit.

After they finished discussing animal shelter business, Frank explained they'd be picking up young Aza at the Simpsons' house because P.W. had gone out of town.

"P.W. never told me how it is he's raising a young boy," Harper said. "I didn't feel I knew him well enough to ask when we drove into Alta, but I take it they're not father and son."

Frank shook his head. "Aza is a relative's kid, and no one else was left in the family who could or would take care of him," he said. "Mother died in childbirth. I don't know anything about the dad. I'm not sure the guy was even aware he fathered a child."

Harper turned down the waitress when she approached and offered to top off her coffee.

Frank was quieter throughout the rest of breakfast, adrift in his thoughts. He and Teresa had been waiting to have children until their careers were established, even though they knew they'd be older parents. If the timing of her death had been postponed by even one year, he might have been the one raising a young boy alone.

Perhaps his relationship with Aza filled in somehow for the child he never had. He knew from watching P.W. grow into the role that parenting was an enormous task.

Frank pulled himself back to present company. "Are you all set, Harper?" he asked. "If so, let's move 'em out."

By the time the pair pulled into the long wooded driveway leading to P.W.'s log home, dark clouds were building.

"Dang weatherman," Frank said, turning off the ignition. "Looks for all the world like a thunderstorm, and there's still snow on the ground. I'll just be a minute fetching Aza."

Harper watched him saunter up the porch steps and let himself into the house with a key. *Nice body,* she thought. Over breakfast she had tactfully asked if he lived alone and learned that Frank was a widower. He did not live alone, however. A pair of inseparable senior dogs from the shelter shared his house. Frank had said he figured the large dogs were too old to find placement together in a single home, but just old enough to be great pets. Harper liked that Frank seemed to have a kind-hearted streak. He called the female Grin and the male, Barrett. That sly sense of humor was appealing too.

Her daydreaming was interrupted when Frank reappeared without Aza and headed to the passenger door.

"Harper, I can't find him anywhere," he said with concern. "I'd leave him a note to call me when he gets back in, but I don't like the looks of this sky. Aza tends to wander quite far afield and could get stuck out in some bad weather."

She exited the truck just as a flash of lightning split the sky and the heavens opened up.

The pair bolted for P.W.'s house.

"What should we do?" Harper yelled as they dashed into the house, dripping water on the floor.

"Fortunately, P.W. taught him to mark his trails so if he leaves the main one he can always find his way back in," Frank said. "Plus I showed him most of the larger trails, ones I explored as a kid. Let's wrestle up some rain gear and see if we can intercept him on his return."

P.W. kept an assortment of foul-weather clothes hanging in the hall closet, so before long the pair were standing in the back yard and looking for the start of Aza's hike.

"Let me just call the pound and tell them we're delayed," Harper said, moving to an overhang along the back of the house. She soon returned and shook her head at Frank. “There’s no answer. I left a message on the machine.”

Frank knew many of Aza’s favorite hikes, and the boy’s footprints and Sheldon’s tracks were easy to spot in the snow that remained on the ground. The unseasonal rain hadn’t washed them all away yet.

“Here,” Frank said over the wind. “Looks like he headed up this way. Watch for any signs that he departed from the main trail as we move along.”

They headed uphill. The nearly freezing rain, though, was rapidly turning the once-solid footing into a field of slush.

Soon Frank regretted having dragged Harper along. Initially he had thought it would be fine to stroll through the forest until they met up with Aza, but this was anything but fun. If he, who could lift a 100-pound dog without strain, was struggling up the slippery slope, he could only imagine what his slightly plump companion was feeling.

After they worked their way single-file through a long rock crevasse with steep sides, he turned to face Harper.

"I'm sorry. I shouldn't have brought you along in these conditions." Frank shouted over the din of the rain. "If you turn back, can you find your way?"

Harper looked at the route they had taken. "I think I can. As they say, it's all downhill."

"Go then," Frank yelled. "That way if somehow we've missed Aza, you'll be there to keep him company until I get back."

"Okay," Harper said, and she turned to go. "Be careful."

The words were barely out of her mouth when a flash lit up the sky, followed instantaneously by a thundering jolt. A pine tree exploded above them and onto the path. Burning branches blocked the retreat to the house.

As the rest of the tree tumbled into the chasm, Frank instinctively grabbed Harper and held her close, shielding her head with his hand and upper body.

"You okay?" he asked, shaking her shoulders lightly to get her to focus. He bent slightly to look directly into her green eyes. "Come on. There's no easy way around that crevasse, now that it's blocked. Let's go with Plan B."

The pair walked briskly quite a ways before slowing down. Frank didn't mean to overtax Harper, but the close call had given him a spurt of energy. He looked back to see that the weather was working in their favor and had quickly extinguished the small flare-up.

"We'll take another trail back and call search and rescue if we don't meet up with Aza," Frank said into Harper's ear. "I know these woods. Aza diverged from the main trail here. But we should intersect another path if we follow his route and be able to turn back in a mile or so. I think there's a trail that will crisscross this one."

"Works for me," Harper said. "I'm officially lost."

The wind was picking up, slinging small branches and pinecones along the route. The temperature was dropping too, but at least the rain had passed. Small trees were bending sideways as gusts buffeted the forest.

Up ahead, Frank saw a wisp of smoke, and

then he smelled burning leaves that he took for marijuana. Illicit growers sometimes planted in fields and meadows deep in the forest where they could farm and harvest in secret. No doubt the remains of one such patch was going up in smoke.

"Smell that?" he asked. "There must be a pot field nearby that got hit by a lightning strike. Stick close to the trail. These illegal plantations are often surrounded by traps."

Stunned, Harper stopped in her tracks. "What plantations?" Her image of the serene spot she had chosen to call home was rapidly disintegrating. She had almost been killed by lightning and a falling tree. Now unseen pot growers presented a threat? She would add this to her list of potential freelance stories.

"Keep moving," Frank shouted back.

Harper hurried to catch up. "I don't want to be the one in the back taken by the zombie," she said as fell in stride beside him. "Why wouldn't the pot growers have harvested all the crop before winter?"

"Oh, sometimes they get scared away by the feds," Frank said. "Could be any number of reasons. There's only about a three-month harvest season. Maybe they got to bring some of it in but not all before the weather turned. We did have a wet fall and early snow-storms. If the plants mold, they're worthless."

Harper was a bit startled by Frank's seemingly extensive knowledge of pot growing. "Is this common in this neck of the woods?" she asked. Frank shrugged. He was focused on following Aza's trail.

The scent of burning marijuana lingered, the leaves giving off a distinct smell. In trying to walk abreast of Frank but not too close, Harper was inadvertently nudging him off the path.

"We should be at the cut-off soon," he said, turning to face her. Then a loud snap rent the air, his face distorted, and he let out a scream of agony. A leghold trap had ensnared his left foot.

5

The forest and darkening sky seemed to close in around Frank. He crumpled onto the slushy ground, gasping to regulate his breath and rocking slightly.

"Oh, my gosh!" Harper said, bending over to grab his shoulders. After several moments of silence she assessed the situation. "We have to get that trap and boot off to see how badly you're injured."

"You think?" Frank said through his clenched teeth. Harper's face stung at the belittling tone of his response. She bit her tongue and reached into her jacket for her cell phone. No signal.

"Ugh," Frank said. "Sorry to take it out on you."

"Apology accepted," Harper said. "You're in

a lot of pain. If this is a pot farm, there may be a shed or something nearby with some tools."

"No. We should stick together. Stand on each spring at the side of the trap and press down hard with your feet. The jaws should relax enough for me to be able to pull my ankle free."

If Harper was aware of the awkwardness of the positions of their bodies, with her crotch practically bumping into Frank's face, she didn't let on. One forceful downward thrust opened the metal jaws. Frank snatched his foot out and rolled onto his side groaning. The trap closed on the empty air with a metallic crack.

"We still need to get this boot off, but not here," he said. Thick wet snowflakes were coming down.

Harper shushed him for a moment while she found a sturdy stick of the appropriate length, and handed the makeshift cane to Frank. "Here. Try this so you don't have to put so much weight on that foot."

Their progress was slow on the uneven ground, with Frank favoring the injured foot and leaning on his walking stick. At least the snowfall was starting to ease up a little. The air was clear and smelled fresh again.

"Let's find a place for me to pull off this boot under a pine canopy," he said. "Keep an eye out."

Frank kept finding traces of Aza's footprints and methodically, if slowly, followed the boy's route through the forest. With the gusty breeze, calling out seemed futile. Periodically, however, there would be a lull in the wind, and Frank blew a whistle he had brought along. He was becoming more concerned as each minute passed. It wasn't like Aza to be late for an outing with Frank. And as much as the boy could be a handful, he was generally responsible about his care of Sheldon. He wouldn't purposefully keep the dog or himself out in this weather.

Soon a clearing under a tree provided a sheltered stopping point where they could inspect Frank's injured foot. He and Harper tucked under the pine boughs and plopped down where the trunk blocked the snowfall. Frank let out a big sigh and stared at the foot. He felt nauseated.

"Shall I do the honors?" Harper asked.

"You can get me started by untying the shoelaces," he said, "but I better be the one to pull off that boot."

With the laces loose, Frank managed to wiggle free, uttering only a few curse words. He almost suggested Harper look away as he removed the sock.

But there it was. One bruised foot – slightly swollen but no skin breaks. Frank was glad he always invested in rugged footwear.

"I better put this boot back on before the thing doesn't fit anymore."

"There's still quite a haul out of here,"

Harper said, trying to figure out how long it had taken them to come this far. "Put your boot on and then raise your leg against the tree for a few minutes before we head off."

"Okay," he said, "but not for too long."

He was cold and tired and thirsty, and they couldn't do a thing to help Aza. Frank silently chastised himself for getting them into this situation. The only option was to press on.

Harper mentally distracted herself from their circumstances by allowing parts of the Requiem to run through her head. From a young age, she often had a tune stuck in her brain. Sometimes she even heard complex orchestral works or the operas that she had listened to over and over again on the family record player. The Germans call the phenomenon ohrwurm, meaning earworm. Supposedly one could shut down an annoying earworm by chewing gum or tapping.

She found the descending notes of the "Agnus Dei" accompaniment particularly soothing. The Latin lyrics translated to "Lamb of God, who taketh away the sins of the world: grant them eternal rest." She felt the warm embrace of the gentle plea. The notes rose again, softly, at the end, and the piece concluded in a quiet unison.

Once they got back on the trail, their progress continued to slow. Frank stopped more frequently, his foot throbbing but functional. Just as he stopped to blow his whistle again they heard a low growl. He and Harper froze in their tracks. What manner of beast had they stumbled upon?

Harper jumped toward Frank and held onto him as if this action would offer some sort of protection. As they exchanged a glance Harper saw Frank's face take on a quizzical expression.

"Sheldon?" Frank shouted. "Aza! Where are you?"

"Here, here," came Aza's reply. "Sheldon's hurt, and I made a fort to protect him."

Aza pushed away the pine branches he had cut and arranged into a makeshift shelter. If Frank had been feeling better he probably would have noticed the hastily built structure up ahead and off to one side of the trail. For her part, Harper had been keeping her eyes on the ground for fear of slipping. Frank hated to think that they might have walked right by if Sheldon hadn't alerted them. What a couple of rescuers they were.

As the pair approached, they saw that Sheldon too had sprung a trap, which encircled his right front paw. Aza had managed to stanch the flow of blood with his scarf, and Sheldon lay on his side, panting heavily.

"That's gotta hurt like hell," Frank said. "Let's get that off. Aza, you hold his head tight while I release the trap. Harper, we're going to need your scarf to tie around the wound. There may be a lot more blood when I pull the trap."

As the boy held the dog, trails of tears rolled down his cheeks. Sheldon whimpered as the trap came off, and Harper quickly wrapped her scarf around the nasty cut, tying it firmly. Frank grabbed Aza in a tight embrace.

"It's okay," he whispered, stroking the top of the boy's head. "He's going to be fine. We're all going to be okay."

The words seemed to dissolve the lad into a puddle of tears, and he sobbed with all his heart. "Oh, honey," Frank said, giving Aza the time he needed to recover from his distress.

"I'm sorry," the boy said at last with a shaking voice. "I'm such a baby."

"You are *not* a baby," Frank said, holding him by the shoulders to look at him face to face.

"Yes, I am," Aza said. "P.W. told me so."

Frank tried to stifle a laugh. "I'm sure he did. And he probably told you a lot of other things. But you stayed with your dog to save his life, out here, all alone in a storm. A baby couldn't do that. Now we're going to get out of here."

But even as he said the words with confidence, his head was awash with the logistics. He couldn't carry the 50-pound dog out on a bad foot, and he doubted Harper or Aza could, either.

"Frank, you don't look at all well," Harper said, bringing him back to the moment. "Why don't you rest while we figure this out?"

She pulled her cell from her pocket and again tried 911. No signal.

"What's the matter with him?" Aza asked, addressing Harper for the first time.

"He stepped into a trap, too," she explained, settling Frank on the ground. "See how his boot is all messed up? Fortunately there's no blood, but his foot is badly bruised and swelling. I think he's a little shocky too, perhaps, but I'm not a medical professional."

"Maybe this will make him feel better," Aza said, pulling his tattered backpack closer from its spot beside the tree. Inside were a cornucopia of snack treats and several bottles of water.

Franks eyes widened and a grin split his ashen face. "How long were you planning to be out this morning?" he asked. "Until New Year's Eve?"

"I get hungry," Aza said defensively. "And P.W. says to always pack in water for Sheldon. Don't let him drink from the puddles or streams."

Harper studied the grimy re-used plastic bottles. "Where did you get this water?" she asked.

"From the tap," he said. "I rinse them out before I fill them."

She noted a few dog hairs floating in the water. "Fair enough." She popped off a top and handed the first bottle to Frank. This was no time to worry about dog germs.

"I'm Harper, by the way," she said in introduction.

Aza seemed to think about that for a while before he spoke. "Are you Frank's girlfriend?"

"Nope," she said, and she laughed. "I'm taking over for Frank at the animal shelter. He's going to show me the ropes."

Aza looked at her with puzzlement. "There are ropes at the shelter?"

"I don't really know." She was reminded of how literal children could be. "That's just an expression."

After the three finished snacking on smashed potato chips, chocolate candies left over from Halloween, and dog water, Frank renewed his assessment of the situation.

"Now, to figure out how to move Sheldon down off this mountain," Frank said, looking from Harper to Aza.

"I already figured that out, Uncle Frankie," Aza said, using a term of endearment he had adopted in recent years. "I was building this sled to get him out. I pull the handles and drag the bottom along the ground. Here."

From behind a tree he produced a crude yet sturdy sled of pine branches tied together with shoe and sweatshirt laces. Frank looked down at Aza's boots and saw they had their laces intact. "You had all that stuff in your backpack too?" he said.

"Sure. Survival stuff."

"You, my young man, *you* are not a baby," Frank said. "I say let's hit that trail. I'm probably feeling as good as I can, considering."

The trio made slow but steady progress with Frank in the lead. Harper and Aza switched off pulling the makeshift sled. That Sheldon was putting up with the indignity of being bumped about on the trek down worried Frank. If anything, the dog seemed too still, too compliant.

Harper was more concerned about Frank's unsteady gait. She put her shoulder under his arm for support while Aza and Sheldon took the lead.

"Maybe you should leave me and send back the cavalry," Frank whispered to Harper.

"Not on your life," she said, trying to buck up his spirits. "We're not leaving you out here for Sasquatch to feast on."

The snow turned into finer flakes as the temperature continued to drop. The sky was darkening even though it was just early afternoon. On one of their many rest stops, Harper finally got a cell signal.

"911. What's your emergency?" asked the operator.

As Harper relayed details and their approximate location, Frank grasped Aza's hand. "If anything had happened to you ...."

Once Harper was off the phone, Frank

punched in the number for the veterinary office that served the community. "Time to call in a favor," he said. "He's got some interns working for him. Perhaps one of them or a vet tech can meet us at P.W.'s place to take Sheldon in right away."

"Should we call P.W.?" Aza asked.

"He doesn't know anything's wrong, so I don't see the need to alarm him," Frank said. "Plus, I'd feel better if we conserved Harper's battery just in case we have to use the phone again."

Buoyed by their reconnection to the outside world, the threesome made better time the rest of the way home. Sheriff's Deputy Jessica Grady met them about a hundred yards from the house.

"Figured you'd find your way home just as I set off to do my Wonder Woman thang," she said, putting her shoulder under Frank's other arm to help him the rest of the way. "Young vet just arrived to take care of that one." She nodded toward Sheldon, whose ramshackle sled was barely holding together.

Frank had never been happier to see Jessica. The two had dated a while back, been lovers in fact, but in the long-term the relationship hadn't worked out. He still found her outdoorsy veneer extremely appealing. The long blond locks emerging from underneath her hat were forming wet strands.

"What a sight for sore eyes and foot," Frank

said, "even looking like a drenched rat. Remind me how you slipped through my fingers."

"Ah," Jessica said. "As far as I recall, I was too much woman for you to handle." The two old friends laughed.

Harper witnessed the exchange with an unexpected mixture of feelings: relief that Frank seemed to be returning to his old self and something else she couldn't quite pinpoint. Jealousy?

Sheldon took center stage for the moment as the vet lifted him gingerly off the sled and onto an animal stretcher he had already set up at the back of the house.

The intern, whose embroidered shirt pocket beneath his open jacket read "Dan-O," inserted an IV in Sheldon's good front paw. Jessica helped him load the animal and tapped the SUV roof twice as he started the engine. "Loaded and locked. Thanks for coming out," she yelled as he sped away.

Inside the house, Frank had collapsed on the sofa with his injured foot elevated on the couch arm. Aza lit the gas fire in the fireplace while Harper conjured up hot cocoa from fixings she found in P.W.'s kitchen.

Jessica returned and surveyed the domestic scene, notebook and pen at the ready. They all seemed to start talking at once.

"So, let me get this straight," she said after extensive note-taking. "Aza took Sheldon for his morning walk. But he failed to meet Frank for their 10 a.m. rendezvous. Frank sets off like Sir Edmund Hillary, dragging along one unsuspecting Harper Henshaw."

"Hey, wait a minute," Frank said. "I resemble that remark."

"Let me continue," Jessica said, holding up her hand and resuming her account. "Both parties stumble upon pot fields mined with leghold traps. Dog and man spring traps. Finally the parties reunite and find their way back, not before calling 911 for assistance."

"Okay," she said. "We'll get the Drug Enforcement Administration out here as soon as possible to clear up that area and collect evidence, if any, about the possible pot operation. Until then, Aza, that particular trail is off-limits."

"Yes, ma'am," he said. Aza sat quietly under a quilt near the fire, biting his lip.

"Aza?" she asked. "You have more to tell me, you better do it now. This is serious federal business."

After a slight hesitation, he spoke. "Well, it's just once I heard some guys up there, and I think someone might have followed me home."

"Here?" Frank asked, nearly shouting.

"Yeah," Aza said. "Another time I thought I saw footprints in the back yard, but then it snowed and they were gone. So then I thought maybe I just 'magined it."

Frank and Jessica exchanged a concerned look.

"I'll let the feds know to put urgent on this one, then," she said. "And a patrol car will be by twice a day, just to keep an eye on things. Thanks for telling me, Aza.

"And as for you, Mr. O'Brien, you've won a free ride to the hospital for some X-rays," she said. "We're a full-service sheriff's department."

"Thanks. Let me call a friend so he can let my dogs out," Frank said, "just in case I end up stuck at the hospital." That task completed, Frank turned to Harper. "Can you manage looking after Aza and taking my vehicle back with you?"

"Sure thing," Harper said. "And I think we better pick up some cheeseburgers on the way to the shelter."

"Yay!" Aza said, brightening considerably.

"Just one more thing, buddy," Jessica said, addressing the boy. "Besides the footprints in the snow, did anything else make you think you might have been followed home? Or anything else unusual happen around that time? Or since then?"

"No," he said, looking back into the flames, where he seemed to ponder the question further. "Just I got in big trouble for something I didn't do."

"And what was that?" she asked.

"P.W.'s keys got lost, and he blamed me."

6

Harper wasted little time cleaning up the cocoa mugs and saucepan. Aza recited P.W.'s cell number, but when Harper dialed it, a phone sitting in the entry hallway rang. So she left a detailed note for P.W., telling him she would keep Aza with her at the shelter until 5 p.m., and then they would head to her house unless she left him a phone message otherwise. She included her address and phone number.

Fortified by take-out burgers and fries from Kelly's, the local drive-through, she and Aza arrived at the animal shelter just as a family with a young girl left carrying a fawn-colored kitten. "Mittens," said the girl brightly. "I'm naming my new kitten Mittens."

"Good for you," Harper said. Adoptions were rapidly becoming her favorite part of working at the facility. They had a near-term beagle mix at the shelter, and Harper was looking forward to the birth of the pups, too.

So far what bothered her most about the job were the dogs crying or shaking in their kennels. A close second was the smell. The mixture of the scents of unbathed dog, urine and feces seemed to cling to her clothing, hair, and particularly the inside of her nose. She could hardly wait to shower or soak in the bathtub each time she had visited the shelter.

P.W. showed up at Harper's house to collect Aza just as she got a call to fetch Frank from the hospital, so they had only a brief exchange.

"I'm sure Aza can tell me all about it," P.W. said, waving her on. "Just go get that fool from the emergency room before he stirs up trouble. Can't let Aza or Frank outta my sight it seems."

After Harper said her goodbyes, she climbed into Frank's late-model truck and turned the ignition key. The engine roared to life. She shivered and adjusted the blower on the heater. Sitting there in quiet solitude while the compartment heated up, the snoop in her took over and she leafed through the contents of the glove compartment: registration, owner's manual, a map, a few pens, receipts, and a granola bar.

Not very enlightening, she thought – kind of like Frank. The man gave the appearance of one in control, who lived an orderly life and was extremely resourceful. But what did she really know about him?

At the hospital, Frank was ready to go. Having lost a battle with a nurse, he greeted Harper from a wheelchair. A prescription bottle was in his lap.

"Don't ask," he said. "This has been one hell of a long day. No broken bones though. I'm ready to go home."

As Frank gave Harper directions to his place, the two talked in snippets about the day's events. "On the drive to the hospital, Jessica told me there has been DEA surveillance in our area for a while now," he said. "They hope to be close to making arrests soon." An involuntary shiver moved up Harper's spine.

"I'd appreciate it if you didn't say anything about our little adventure to anyone from the church or choir, or I'll never get any rest," Frank said. "The tale will get around sooner or later, and parishioners will be pounding down my door, bringing casseroles."

Harper pledged her secrecy.

Just before they reached St. Cross, Frank instructed Harper to turn up a winding drive lined with pine trees. His house stood on a rise, sheltered in back by mature trees. A wide veranda across the front of the structure and a glowing porch light gave the home a welcoming appearance. The moon was already up above the horizon.

A chorus of joyful barking erupted from inside the house as Harper pulled in next to a U.S. Forest Service vehicle and cut the engine.

"They'd recognize the sound of the truck anywhere," Frank said. "Be prepared for an enthusiastic greeting."

Two dogs and Hans Nilsson, the friend Frank had called earlier, met them at the door.

"Just had these beasts out," said the tall Scandinavian-looking man. He was covered in dirt and wearing a soiled work uniform of dark green slacks and a khaki-colored shirt with a pine tree emblem. "But they haven't eaten yet."

Frank struggled into the living room and seemed in no shape to handle introductions.

"I'm Hans," his friend said, extending a grimy hand to Harper. He spoke with a vaguely European accent.

"Harper," she said, caught off guard by the strength of his grip.

Next, the dogs appraised Harper with their noses, sniffing her pants and boots as though reading a newspaper of the day's events. After helping settle Frank on his couch, Hans turned to apologize to Harper.

"Sorry I've got to run," he said. "I've got to

clean up for a date. And Frank looks like he's in good hands. Nice to meet you, Harper. I hope we can get better acquainted another time." He had a sincerity about him that Harper liked.

She said goodbye, closed the front door, and crossed the room to light the fireplace. The house was chilly after standing empty all day.

Curious about their visitor, the canines followed Harper into the kitchen and watched while she filled their bowls. Hans had left the kibble out and already replenished their water. Dogs fed, Harper checked on Frank in the living room before going back to the kitchen to scavenge for the makings of a meal. "You should probably have something to eat," she yelled over her shoulder.

On the couch, Frank drifted in and out of his thoughts and emotions. The pain meds he had been given at the hospital seemed to be messing with his mind. He, Harper, Aza, or Sheldon might have lost their lives earlier that day and, as relieved as he was, his focus kept returning to Jessica Grady. She would definitely make the short list of "great loves" in his life. But that hadn't worked out, he reminded himself. Seeing her had rekindled some warm feelings, however – perhaps not all particularly about her, but about companionship, partners, and being in love.

His eyes rested on the portrait of his wife on the mantelpiece. How different his life might have been, if .... He tried to push the event out of his mind, but once again the haunting scene replayed itself.

The new day had started like so many others in that part of paradise. The morning mist was burning off in the canyons and valleys, and the sun was already heating up the granite faces of the Sierra Nevada Mountains.

"Fine time for a hike," Frank had said upon rising. "Let's have a quick breakfast and head out." Teresa agreed. The household chores could wait.

Their rustic house was near the popular Edison Falls trailhead. Soon they were rising steadily through the ponderosa and Jeffrey pine canopy. The winter snows were melting, and icy water was filling the rocky streambeds. The nearby waterfall was their destination. The gushing cascade would be especially showy in the early light. Mountain chickadees filled the forest with sound, interrupted only by the couple's footfalls and intermittent conservation.

Frank studied Teresa's form as he followed her up the mountain. "The footing is getting a little treacherous through here," she shouted back. "Watch yourself."

He took in the curve of her hips; the shape of her calves, pale from a winter in long pants; the way her waist nipped in. Absentmindedly, he fingered the gold band on his left hand. He had a callus where the ring rubbed against the flesh of his palm. A smile creased his face as he took in the moment. He felt so grateful – for his life, his wife, for their good fortune to be able to live close to such natural beauty.

The sound of distant water interrupted his thoughts. "I love you," he said. She turned back briefly and smiled.

Frank wanted to reach out and touch Teresa – to hold her in an embrace. But they'd be at the base of the falls soon enough, and there would be plenty of time for that. They continued their steady uphill pace.

Frank felt the rumble before he realized what was happening. His feet faltered, and he grabbed at a nearby tree. "Careful," he yelled.

Up ahead, Teresa moved to steady herself with a hand on a rock outcropping, waiting for the earthquake to subside. Loose stone falling from high above began pelting the path.

Frank felt the sapling to which he was anchored shiver as a small boulder clipped off the top of the tree. "Mother of God!" he said, and fell to the ground. The rock had narrowly missed him.

By the time the shaking stopped, Frank was

spitting out dust. “Teresa,” he yelled. He got to his hands and knees and yelled again. “Teresa!” At last on his unsteady feet, he tried again. “TERESA!”

He could hear rocks still skittering down the hillsides, but no reply. Rounding the curve in the trail, he reached her. She was motionless. The side of her head, with its lovely brunette hair, was wet with blood.

Frank grabbed her wrist to feel for a pulse. As he held her, the beat flickered away. Frank pulled the loose stones from around her, heaving them off the trail and screaming, looking for the culprit. But the rock had already moved on down the hillside, a fresh red mark on one side. Finally, he had collapsed with a moan of anguish as his world caved in around him.

Teresa’s death had taken a huge toll on Frank. Then the aftermath had prolonged his grief. An over-zealous coroner had conjectured that Frank might have used the earthquake as a cover to bash in his wife’s skull with a handy rock. “Yes, I moved a small boulder to reach her.” “No, I did not hit her with a piece of granite.” The inquest that followed had left his emotions in shreds.

Of course, the investigation found no evidence of wrongdoing. Nevertheless, Frank felt vilified by the system and even by some members of the community. As he again pondered her death, so long ago, it struck him that most of

St. Cross' current residents were unaware that Teresa ever existed. Frank, however, thought of her every day.

"God, I miss that woman," he said.

"Pardon me, Frank?" Harper asked. She was just coming into the living room with a simple supper on a tray.

"Oh, nothing," he said with a crack in his voice. Frank felt a bit chagrinned to be coming apart emotionally in front of his new acquaintance.

Harper cocked her head to one side and gave him an inquisitive look. "Don't you 'oh, nothing' me," she said, trying to keep the conversation light. "We barely know each other."

"Well, then, come in here, woman," he said with a false bravado borne of the pain medication. He thumped his hand on the empty spot on the couch. Suddenly he didn't want to be alone. "Feed me my dinner, and let's see what we can do about that."

Harper thought of her cold and dark bungalow. Tempted as she was to remain in the cozy living room, she was exhausted from the eventful day. Her claw-foot tub was beckoning.

"Raincheck on that, Roger," she said. "You can feed yourself and then sleep off whatever pain med high you're on." She put the dinner tray within easy reach and returned with a fresh glass of water for him.

"Seriously, if you think you'll be okay, I'll just steal your truck and head on home. I'm beat."

"No problem," Frank said. "I'll get P.W. to drop me over there tomorrow. I can pick it up then. My cell's in the entryway. Would you mind putting your phone and address in my contacts? I know I found your house once before, but I think these meds are giving me brain damage."

She assented and turned to leave.

"And Harper?" Frank said. "Thanks for today. You were a real trooper out there."

7

P.W. stepped onto Frank's porch after Sunday services. He pounded on the front door.

"Hey, lazybones," he shouted from the chilly stoop. "Let's get this show on the road."

"Coming, dear," Frank said. He was hobbling along better after 12 straight hours of sleep. "Where's Aza?" he asked as he opened the door.

"Packed him off to a friend's after church," P.W. said. "Kid's mom knows her way around a snickerdoodle cookie. They'll be having big-time adventures in baking this afternoon. What the hell happened yesterday?"

Frank told his version of the day's misadventures during the ride to Harper's bungalow. P.W. told Frank that the vet's office had called to say that Sheldon was resting and receiving IV fluids.

"So, your entire set of keys went missing a

month ago?" Frank asked. His mind kept coming back to this detail.

"Didn't think much of it," P.W. said with a shrug. "Figured Aza played with them on one of his imaginary adventures and lost them somewhere in the woods. Claimed he didn't, but I didn't believe him. Stubborn boy would not give up that story."

"But what if Aza is telling the truth? Maybe someone from the pot operation *did* follow him home and steal your keys," Frank said. "They'd have keys to the church, your truck, the house. You didn't have a shelter key, did you?"

"Now don't you start that with me," P.W. said. "No wonder the boy has such a vivid imagination. Spends too much time with Uncle Frankie. Besides, it's just a handful of keys. They weren't labeled."

Frank mulled that fact. "Still, I'm changing all the church keys as soon as I can get a locksmith out," he said. They pulled into Harper's driveway. Her car was gone.

"Speaking of keys," Frank said, "how am I going to break into my truck?"

P.W. reached into his pocket to hoist Frank's keychain into the air. "She passed these to me between the Prayer of Confession and the Offering," he said.

"No she didn't," Frank said, snatching the keys away. "You, old man, are incorrigible."

P.W. reached behind his seat and produced a dozen red roses wrapped in cellophane. Frank gave him a surprised look. "What the – "

"Simmer down, Sir Edmund," P.W. said. Apparently Aza had been quite thorough in his recitation of yesterday's events. "Aza and I want to thank the lady proper-like. You both went above and beyond. Aza is safe. Sheldon should heal. Just because you may have forgotten your manners doesn't mean we have. You owe Harper a proper thank you yourself."

P.W. seemed to be quite happy hassling Frank, so he kept at it.

"Why, Aza says you two would make a right cute couple," P.W. said. "I think sometimes he worries that I'm getting up there in years, and he knows that, legally, you are the back-up plan. Maybe he fantasizes about having a mom one day."

"Over-imagination must run in your family," Frank said, trying to make light of the comment. But P.W. *was* "getting up there," wherever that was. He understood Aza's concern. They had explained to the boy that, should anything ever happen to P.W., Frank would be his guardian. He hadn't thought about Aza longing for a mother.

As Frank slowly navigated his way to the truck, P.W. reverently laid the bouquet on Harper's front stoop. The deep red of the flowers stood out against the polished wooden door.

Those roses are not such a bad idea, Frank admitted to himself as he revved his engine and waved to P.W. *Wish I had thought of it first.*

8

Harper sipped her morning coffee and watched the fog dissipate in a canyon she could see from her dining room table. She'd loved the fog since moving to St. Cross. The blanket of moisture was a welcome relief from the usually dry air of the Sierras. She studied the crimson roses, which she had placed in a vase on the table, and tried to calm her thoughts.

For days she had been reliving the trauma of the trek in the snowstorm. The event invaded her dreams and waking hours. Harper even found herself cringing when she clanked her pots and pans together in the sink, recalling the metal-on-metal sound the trap made when Frank had pulled his foot out.

Her cell rang. She snatched it up.

"Gene," she said without preamble to her longtime friend and editor.

"Feeling any better?"

"Not really. The memory of the lightning strike is the worst. I'm still jumpy."

"Understandable."

"I'm not sure why that image is so unnerving. It's as though God reached down with sound, light, and fury to get my attention – and succeeded."

"That was a close call. Anyone would have been terrified."

"Ugh!" she said, frustrated at her mental state. "St. Cross is turning out to be such an unsettling place to live. What have I gotten myself into?"

"Harper, don't be so hard on yourself. You had a really bad day that brought home the fact that you are living in what is essentially wilderness – with a whole set of new and different dangers compared to urban life. On top of that, your bargain-priced house has expensive problems. That can happen to anyone, anywhere.

"You've taken on a lot by moving to a new area. But you will settle in. Give yourself time. On the upside, sounds like you'll have one helluva good story for me about marijuana growing and a steady stream of interesting pitches. Illegal pot plantations on U.S. forestlands? That's an editor's dream."

"Well, it's one tough way to get a story," she said. "You're right that there's some upside, though. I am grateful to still be alive."

Although she said nothing about it to Gene, Harper also was aware that she felt a newfound closeness to Frank from the shared ordeal. To her disappointment, however, there were no indications that he felt the same way.

All business, Frank had texted her Tuesday to reschedule their missed session at the shelter. Then he'd texted her soon after dawn this morning to ask for a ride to this evening's choir practice. Apparently his truck had hose problems, and he needed to pick up some parts on the way. Plus, he'd had the locksmith in to change the fittings at the church and wanted to arrive early to make sure everything was in order for the rehearsal.

Harper filtered out the parts she chose to keep from Gene. If he thought she was developing a crush on some mountain man, she'd never hear the end of it. "I am less shaken than I was several days ago, but it's like processing in a vacuum up here. My style is to share and talk about things."

She was disappointed by Frank's radio silence. He would have been the perfect person with whom to compare notes and work through her emotions.

"That's why we have social media and

long-distance – so there's community everywhere," Gene said.

"I do appreciate the call," she said. "I feel like I dragged through this entire week and have nothing to show for it."

"Hang in there, Harper. Just because you can't show anything for your time doesn't mean it wasn't valuable. I know it sounds cliché, but this too shall pass."

"Such a sage. Thanks, Gene."

Off the phone, Harper returned to her rapidly cooling coffee. The beverage, so comforting at first, seemed to be burning the base of her throat. She recognized the symptom of self-doubt. *Frank just needs a ride,* she thought. *And that's all. Don't get your hopes up.*

Somehow men just didn't think of her as someone they wanted to date. They never had.

Harper found the antacid in her aged medicine cabinet and popped two of the chalky tablets in her mouth. After running her fingers through her hair, she headed out the door for her day at the animal shelter.

With Frank out of commission, longtime staffer Vivian Weaver was bringing Harper up to speed on most of the day-to-day duties. The older woman was just flipping the "CLOSED"

sign to "OPEN" when Harper pulled into the parking lot.

"Good morning," Vivian shouted at Harper from the door. "You're just in time for fresh coffee."

Harper hustled in out of the cold. "Normally I would welcome that offer, but I seem to have overdosed already this morning."

She hung her coat on a peg. There was something she'd been meaning to ask. It was time to clear the air.

"Vivian, doesn't it seem strange for you to be teaching me how to do this job? You already know how to do it. You're much better equipped."

"No, thank you – although I do appreciate the compliment. My husband Leonard has Parkinson's and requires way too much of my attention. Part-time work is all I want. Don't worry. You can do this. I've got your back."

"I'm just not sure how I feel about running the show here," Harper said. "As much as I would prefer to sit in the front and act as administrator, there seems to be a constant stream of odd jobs that call me to the back. Many times I just feel so inadequate to the task."

"Most everyone here felt that way at first. Those of us who look like we know what we're doing, like me and Buck? We've been at it for years."

Despite the assurances, Harper remained unconvinced. Could she collar a dog to take it out of a kennel without the animal slipping past her and escaping? Would the largest ones get the better of her and pull her over? What if she were bitten?

The fact that the St. Cross facility was a private, "no kill" shelter meant they could refuse any animals they considered unadoptable. None were put down on site. There was no guarantee, however, that animals passing through their doors would not eventually end up at the County shelter and be euthanized. The "no kill" misrepresentation bothered Harper.

She took her place at the reception desk and booted up the outdated computer. Vivian was sorting through some paperwork that would require Harper's attention.

"It's just I've always been so certain of myself as a reporter," Harper said. "I can string words together because I control them – the selection, the order, the emphasis." Animals were another matter altogether – unpredictable, potentially dangerous, sometimes beyond hope or repair.

Vivian plopped a stack of papers in front of Harper. "Yes, ma'am. Now wade through these community service applications while I go attend to some things in the back. Sammie will be in this afternoon, and I'm gonna line up some chores for her to do."

Darkness fell before Harper closed up the shelter for the day. After a quick bite to eat from Kelly's, she turned up Frank's driveway and spied him waiting on his front porch. Using a cane, he hobbled to her sedan and opened the passenger-side door. A duet of barking could be heard from inside his house.

Frank sat beside her. "Great to see you again, Harper." He smiled and patted her arm. "Sorry to call you out of your way, but I haven't had a chance to talk to you in person since I banged up my foot, so I thought this might be a good chance to catch up. There's something I wanted to tell you."

This was not what Harper had expected. Frank had her full attention. After turning the car around in his driveway, she pulled to a stop near the street and faced him.

He took a swallow and met her eyes. "I owe you a lot for your help Saturday. I put you in danger, and I'm sorry. I hope I can return the favor someday."

A smile spread across Harper's face even as she realized Frank's countenance was serious. She tilted her head and noticed his eyes were hazel. He was looking down, seeming to study her car floor mat.

"It's just," Frank said, "I lost my wife years ago hiking in these mountains. I still think that I might have somehow prevented the accident. Then when that tree almost took you out .... I so regretted bringing you along. I felt like I was reliving a nightmare."

Harper reached across the console and touched Frank's forearm. Then she put the car in drive, turned onto the road, and focused on her driving. Everything she thought to say seemed inadequate or even patronizing. She had no words to offer him, only her presence. In her experience, grieving was often silent work – an individual pursuit – but there was comfort in just having someone else there. So she gave him space, and let his words linger in the air between them.

After a quiet ride and brief stop at Carlos' Auto Repair, they pulled into the church parking lot. Despite their early arrival, Harper and Frank weren't the first people there. Right outside the doors to the narthex, parked beside the Frasiers' SUV, was a black-and-white with lights flashing. The uniformed officer, who stood with arms akimbo, was none other than Jessica.

9

At the sight of a brick-sized hole in the stained-glass of the church's front door, Frank excused himself. He thought he'd better tell Jessica about his suspicions that small things had seemed out of place at the church lately.

Harper, feeling somewhat superfluous with her duties as chauffeur completed, headed directly into the choir room.

The events of the early evening were all the buzz.

"Adam and Mimi got here first to find a gaping crack in the front door where a hand bell had shattered the stained-glass," said choir know-it-all Judy. "Then Debbie Benes pulled up, and she called 911."

For once, Adam missed his 7:20 downbeat. Throughout rehearsal, he seemed quite out of sorts. Mimi appeared unwell. The singers could barely focus on their scores. Church board members who sang in the chorus whispered back and forth.

"We should hold an emergency meeting after practice," Kevin Cheema said to his fellow bass P.W.

"No," P.W. said. "Give it until tomorrow, when we may know more. Then we'll firm up the meeting plans." The cost to repair the decorative glass door would be astronomical. Nothing could be decided without more information.

Perhaps Harper alone got into the music that evening. Singing often made her feel better when she was in a slump. She sometimes felt practically giddy as she sang. That night was one of those times. Her brain was releasing endorphins, and she had to fight hard to remain still.

For the first time anyone could remember, the director ended rehearsal early. Sammie, from her perch in the soprano section, breathed a sigh of relief. "Yes," she whispered.

This meant Sammie had free time her parents knew nothing about. Nearly an hour to chat up the college students, walk to the convenience store, or do whatever she wanted – unsupervised.

As she picked her way down the practice room tiers in her tight jeans and heels, Jim from the bass section motioned to her.

"Hey," he said, "how about that ride back to school? Offer still stands."

Sammie took a deep breath and drew herself up to her full five-foot, six-inch stature. "About that," she said. "I guess I didn't make myself clear last week. I don't actually go to your college. I go to the local high school. I should have said."

"Really?" Jim replied. "Well, you look like you could go to my college. I'm just a freshman so we're practically the same age, I bet. Tell you what. Since we're out early how about we go to the drive-through for a snack, then I'll drop you home before I head back to school."

Sammie couldn't believe her good fortune. "I'd love that!"

The two made easy conversation on the way to Kelly's. Before long they were drinking ice cold root beers and sharing an order of fries. "I'm toying with the idea of majoring in anthropology," Jim said, "but I'm not sure that'll be my final choice. I'm having a hard time seeing the connection between subjects that interest me and how they translate into a career."

Sammie nodded and ran a soggy fry through the mound of ketchup on their paper tray. "I recently started volunteering at the animal shelter, and now all I can think about is vet school. But my undergraduate grades would have to be way better than my high school marks for that to happen."

By the time they were done eating, Sammie needed to get back home. It was a quick ride to her house.

"Why don't you drop me here, just down the street from my place," she said. "My parents .... "

"No problem," Jim said. "I get it." He pulled up to a dark spot along the road.

"Thanks," Sammie said, putting her hand on the passenger-side door handle.

"Wait," Jim said. He grabbed her wrist and then leaned in to plant a rough kiss on her lips.

Sammie felt a rush of desire. Soon their tongues were probing each other's mouths. After a few minutes, they pulled away from each other.

"I better go," Sammie said. This was nothing like the awkward pecks and fawning she had endured from high school boys. She felt weak.

"Yeah," Jim said. "See you next Thursday."

Sammie flew in the front door and raced up the stairs, with just the barest greeting to her folks.

"Wow," she said to her reflection in the bathroom mirror. "Just wow." Something odd was happening "down there." She smiled. This was new territory.

10

P.W. called an emergency meeting of the church board for noon. As usual, the estate of Edith Saint Cross was picking up the catered lunch tab. Edith's generosity always ensured a good turnout at church meetings.

After the board assembled, Frank made quick work of passing the gavel to the new chairman. "P.W. Simpson," he said, "you know Debbie from choir. She's our clerk and will keep you in line about Robert's Rules. I now dub you the Big W, and I hope that nickname sticks. You have the floor, sir."

Once other formalities had been dispensed with, P.W. updated the board members on the stained-glass door incident. The sheriff's department had taken the hand bell into evidence and found fingerprints on it. Because there were several sets of prints on the bell, Officer Grady was coming in later in the meeting to fingerprint and eliminate those people who would legitimately have been handling the bells.

"She should take mine," Debbie said. "That's one of the bells I play."

Adam shifted in his chair. "Mine, too," he said.

P.W. cleared his throat and continued. "There seems to be a concern that the church might have been used by drug dealers," he said. "Some keys went missing from my house a while back, and then Aza and Frank discovered a pot field way up beyond my place. Aza thought he was trailed home once. I just put it up to the boy's imagination."

The normally chatty committee was silent. These details were much more sinister than anyone had imagined.

Adam wasn't one to miss an opening. "So drug dealers may have been using our church facilities to distribute?" he asked, aghast. "Really, that is too shoddy, Mr. Simpson. You've put us all in danger. Why, Mimi or I are sometimes here at all hours."

P.W. sat mutely, and Frank responded. "We don't know that this has anything to do with drug dealers, although some clues seem to be stacking up that way," he said. "Fortunately I changed all the locks when I heard about P.W.'s missing set of keys. The broken window happened after the new locks were in, so perhaps whoever wanted to gain entry was thwarted."

Harold Yukata raised his hand from the far end of the conference room table, where his sandwich sat untouched.

"None of this really makes much sense," he said, looking from Frank to P.W. "Someone stealing a hand bell and then returning it through a window sounds more like vandalism. Something teenagers or middle-schoolers might do – or perhaps even a disturbed parishioner."

Several heads around the table nodded in agreement.

"Well, the only teen to come near this music program is that Sammie Hernandez," Adam said. "The college students were all vetted by me and are singing the Requiem for extra credit. I doubt they'd have any sort of grudge against the church. And I'm not failing anyone, so the act can hardly have been directed at me."

Harold continued his line of reasoning. "But few others would have access to the choir room and the bells. Didn't that bell turn up missing on a Thursday?"

Adam pondered Harold's point. "True," he said. "The discovery was made on a Thursday. I happen to know, and this is for our ears only, that Samantha joined the Requiem choir as some sort of punishment. Her mother told me

Sammie would be joining us, but she didn't go into why."

Kevin Cheema piped up. "I don't know her family. Does anyone here know them? They've never been churchgoers, as far as I can recall."

This time the heads around the table moved from side to side.

Not one to put stock in gossip or speculation, P.W. tabled further discussion of Sammie and picked up where the hastily compiled agenda had left off. "Since we are facing unexpected costs with the stained-glass repair, the board should know that the estate of Edith Saint Cross has had to adjust some areas of church spending.

"Unfortunately, the stock market battered our source of funds. Budgets for music, maintenance and outreach are all cut by 20 percent, effective immediately – salaries, though, remain intact."

Adam rose to protest.

"No, dagnabbit," P.W. said. "Don't start. I don't make the rules, I just carry them out to the best of my ability. You'll have to rein in on paid orchestra and soloists or figure out how to fundraise the difference."

A rap on the door brought their attention to Officer Grady, who stood in the hallway, waiting to fingerprint whoever might have been handling the bells. Debbie and Adam followed her out.

P.W. adjourned the meeting, and the remaining board members turned their attention to their lunches. Frank had just finished cleaning up after the meal when Jessica popped her head back into the conference room.

"Get anything?" Frank asked.

"Well," she said, "we think there are possibly two partial sets of prints on the bell. We'll see if Debbie or Adam account for any of them. Debbie says she is good about always handling the bells wearing gloves. If so, we may not get a match for her. Larger prints seem to be smudging out the smaller prints in two spots. Makes me think a man, or a woman with very large hands, was the last person to touch the bell. What bothers me is that two of the three people who were first on the scene may have their prints on the bell. Coincidences never sit well with me. I'm going back to the office to get these to the technicians. Then I may head back out to talk to Debbie and go over her version of events again."

Frank's eyes lighted on Jessica's open face, noting where some errant blond hairs had worked their way out of her braid to form a crown of sorts around her head. "You go, girl," he said. But she was already turning to leave.

11

After the unsettling incidents in the mountains and at the church, Harper dove into her new work life at the animal shelter. She wanted to feel grounded in some activity – any activity – outside the swirl of recent unpredictable events.

Working at the shelter took her mind off her mounting home-repair bills and her growing attraction to Frank. He was showing no signs that the feeling was mutual. And yet, they did seem to be becoming friends. *I can use all of those I can get,* Harper thought, as she hosed out a kennel.

Vivian jarred her from her musings. "Mrs. Henshaw," she said.

"Harper, call me Harper, Vivian," she replied. "There's no mister anymore. I went back to my maiden name."

"We have two intakes on the way, Harper Vivian," Vivian said in jest. "Canine. Sheriff's deputies are bringing them down from the pot operation up behind P.W.'s place. And you can just call me Vi."

Harper grinned at the joke, then tore off her gloves and handed them to Vi, along with the hose. "I guess you win this chore."

By the time Harper got two kennels outfitted with food, water, and bedding, a pair of unmarked cars was pulling into the lot where newcomers were dropped off by animal control or law enforcement agencies. The public generally used the front entrance.

A sinewy DEA agent popped out of the first car and extended his hand. "Jorge Delgado," he said. "Can you hold these two until County picks them up? Evidence dogs."

Harper hadn't dealt with an evidence hold before, but she knew these dogs weren't going out of the shelter adopted. They'd be kept until the investigative work was mopped up before they had a chance of landing homes.

A Presa Canario mix was drooling on the back window of the agent's car. "Yeah," Harper said, assessing the size of the leash she was carrying. "Just let me get a bigger one of these."

She returned with a sturdier leash and Buck, one of her strongest kennel workers. Despite the dog's broad head and large body, it was weak and gave little resistance to the transfer inside.

The Staffordshire terrier mix in the next vehicle was more difficult. Apparently this one was not a fan of men and snapped at Buck. After much coaxing with a gentle voice and treats, Harper was able to leash the emaciated dog and lead it inside. Neither dog looked healthy.

"Vet'll be by to do DNA testing and check them out," Jorge said.

"DNA testing?" Harper asked. She envisioned drug enforcement agents making bets on the results. I told you that was a Presa Canario, one would say, sweeping up several $20 bills from a table.

"Yep," Jorge said. "Department uses it all the time. Dogs leave shit, pardon the expression ma'am, everywhere, and these dogs had owners. They appear to have been guard dogs at the pot operation and were found wandering the site when we moved in."

Harper found it appalling that anyone would abandon their dogs. After the agent signed the necessary forms, he was on his way.

She looked in on both animals and decided it was a good time to call Frank. Her list of questions was growing longer by the minute. He picked up on the first ring.

"So, I can't take them out on walks?" she asked. "No interaction with volunteers?"

"Nope, nothing," Frank said. "That's why they call it an evidence hold. You hold them. You feed 'em, you water them. You can let them into the yard for a stretch. Only staff interacts with these dogs. They aren't going anywhere other than County, which usually takes its time when the animals are already secured. In the meantime, the shelter is paid a per diem to hold them."

Harper mulled over the information for a while with the dawning realization that it was unlikely these dogs would ever become anyone's pets. "Frank," she said, "doesn't this seem like a lot of law enforcement activity just for some pot growing?"

"Yeah," he said, "I've been thinking the same thing. Jessica, uh, Officer Grady hinted that what we found was part of something larger than a single pot-growing operation. This is way beyond what local law enforcement can handle. The DEA is obviously on to something."

Harper felt no more secure here than she had living in the city. Was there no safe haven where people could simply live out their quiet lives?

I've been such a fool, she thought, remembering the life and ties she left behind. The escape she sought seemed to have led her into another whole set of problems instead.

"So is that a yes?" Frank asked. "You're not saying anything."

"Pardon me?" Harper asked. "I'm sorry. Got lost in my thoughts."

"Dinner? Tonight? My place?" he said. "I'm cooking."

A grin pushed her cheeks up toward her eyes. "Sure," she said. "Just tell me the time and what kind of wine to bring."

Once off the phone, Harper went in search of Sammie. She found the teenager in the grooming room, brushing out the coat of an ancient-looking Welsh corgi.

"Stray?" Harper asked, raising an eyebrow.

"Owner surrender," Sammie said, continuing to brush the animal with gentle rhythmic strokes. "Mrs. Zelinsky had to be hospitalized, and she can't care for Delilah anymore."

"Hum," Harper said, looking at the quiet bundle of fur. If she wasn't careful, she'd take them all home. "Sammie, can you do me a favor? I need to duck out 30 minutes before closing. Night staff will be in the back checking on the inmates – er, guests. I need a front-desk person for that half-hour. Do you mind?"

"No, not at all," Sammie said. "I was done here anyway."

Harper was taken aback by the girl's cheerful helpfulness. Was this the same Sammie Hernandez who was skulking about head down when she first met her?

"Sammie," Harper said, seizing the moment,

"what are you in here for anyway?" Hearing the prison reference, the teen laughed out loud, whipping her shimmering black hair away from her face. At least half the shelter "volunteers" were there doing community service, mostly for DUIs.

"Idiot parents," she said as she hoisted the corgi and placed it carefully into a kennel. "Some doofus from school sent me a dick pic, and my mom saw it when she supposedly 'just picked up' my phone."

"What? A dick pic?" Harper asked. "Is that what I think it is?"

"What else would it be," Sammie said, some of her snarky veneer returning. "Like I would want anything to do with those immature high school boys, always begging for nude photos. And my folks wonder why I hate school. My parents are clueless. It's college for me and outta St. Cross as soon as I can."

Harper felt taken aback. "I guess I'm pretty clueless too. Is this what goes on in high schools these days?"

"Try middle school, too," Sammie said. "It's a screwed system for the girls. If you won't send nudes you're a prude. If you do, you're a slut. Personally, I'd just prefer to be invisible on all social media. Maybe my folks did me a favor by taking away my phone. At least I don't know what people are saying about me now."

Harper, who had always identified herself as a feminist, let the information sink in. "I'm sorry," she said. "Sexism and the double standard seem to be alive and well."

Sammie looked at her and shrugged. "It's nothing to do with your generation," she said.

"Is it that bad?" Harper asked.

The teenager nodded. "One girl in my class couldn't take it anymore and tried to hang herself. She didn't die, but she never came back to school."

"I guess my head has been in the sand," Harper said. "I've been so busy beefing about wage equity, glass ceilings, and other women's issues involving my age group that it never occurred to me that my younger sisters might be going through anything like this. I'm sorry things seem to have gotten worse instead of better. We were so self-consumed that we've ignored your generation."

Sammie plopped down at the reception desk. "Pfft," she said. "Whatever. I wouldn't lose any sleep over it."

Once Harper was on a line of questioning, she didn't let up. She might be officially off the news desk, but her inquisitive nature remained. "Why didn't you just tell your parents that the photo was unsolicited? That you were being sexually harassed?"

Sammie stared at her as though wings had

suddenly sprouted from Harper's head. "Is that what you call it? Sexual harassment? Sheesh. That's just standard high school shit. Anyway, they wouldn't have bought that. Obviously I must have 'done something' for him to send the photo." Sammie let her hands stay up where she had air-quoted the words. "They would probably say it was because of the way I dress."

"And what about the church?" Harper asked, continuing in reporter mode since Sammie was still talking. "Is singing in the choir part of your 'sentence'?"

"Ha," Sammie said. "Fooled my folks on that one. I happen to like singing, and I think some of those college kids are pretty cool. It's not so bad."

"So, would you normally go to church?" Harper asked. "I don't see other high-schoolers in the choir."

"Oh, I used to go when my grandmother was alive," Sammie said, "when I was little. But not since she died. My folks never went. Church was just a special thing for the two of us."

"Do you miss it?" Harper asked. "Going to church?"

"Not really." Sammie shrugged. "Kind of seems like fairytale stuff to me now. I mean, who gives up a perfect life to eat an apple? Hello."

"But do you believe in God?" Harper asked.

"I don't know," Sammie said. "I did when

I was a little kid. My grandmother made God seem so real. Kind of like my folks made Santa Claus and the Easter Bunny seem real, but more serious. Maybe church is just for old people and children. I mean, Gramma was old and had a vested interest in believing in God ... just in case."

Harper thought about what Sammie was saying. "Just in case God and heaven really exist?" she asked. "I think God does mean different things to different people as they go through life's stages. A mystery that reveals more and more of itself with time. Just try to stay open to it, Sammie."

"Whatever," said the teen, signaling that she, at least, was done with the conversation.

Harper decided it was time to make her exit. She'd need every minute to pick up the wine and get ready for dinner tonight.

Sammie doodled on the desk calendar. Maybe Jim would stop in and surprise her, she thought. But then again, probably not.

Her smart phone remained under "house arrest," as her dad had proclaimed. She had, however, signed into her social media accounts from a computer at the library when she was supposed to be researching a paper. Sammie had friended Jim and was dismayed to see lots of pictures of him with a tall blonde. His relationship status read: "It's complicated."

She watched the minutes tick by on the wall clock.

At 5:45 p.m. the door jingled open and a slight man with a goatee entered. As he approached the desk, she could see his muscled arms were covered in what she would call "tribal tats." A geometric pattern ran up his right forearm.

"I'm lookin' for a dog," he said, lifting his sunglasses to look her up and down.

She immediately sat up straighter and put on her "don't even think about messing with me" face.

"Would you like to adopt or are you looking for a missing dog?" she asked, the picture of professionalism.

"Just looking," he said with a lecherous smirk, "for a bitch."

Sammie pressed the intercom. She knew "bitch" was another word for a female dog and was determined not to let this guy get to her. Who had Harper said was manning the back? "Any staff to the front desk please," she said. Her visitor paced the floor and kept an eye on the front windows. Finally, after several more tries, Buck responded to her page.

"I'm up to my eyeballs in ... something ... back here." His voice crackled through the outdated system. "Whatcha need?"

"Visitor wants to see the dogs, but I can't leave the desk," she said.

"I can't help ya. Just lock the front door and come on back," he said. "Anyone else comes they'll either knock or go away. We don't usually get many this near to closing."

Sammie was relieved to hear Buck's voice. She hadn't gotten to know him and generally steered clear of old men. He was easily in his mid-30s.

But more than one thing about this visitor was giving her the creeps. She sprang to her feet and turned the deadbolt on the front door, then motioned for the man to follow her into the kennel area. Thinking better of that, she let him pass through the inner door first. Sammie didn't want his eyes on her butt.

She trailed as the man hurried past the kennels. He stopped at the last two.

"What about these?" he asked, gesturing to the evidence-hold dogs. The brindle terrier cried softly, and the larger dog lay still with its head between its paws, plastered to the floor.

Sammie surveyed the red tags on the kennels' paperwork. She hadn't seen the scarlet marks used before, but she knew what they meant: hold. "They aren't available for adoption," she said.

"Humph," the dark-haired man responded and tugged on his goatee. He turned to leave. "Why?"

"I don't know," she said, impatience showing in her voice. "They just aren't. Something to do with police business."

He left without another word.

12

Harper managed to shower, change, and stop for wine on her way to Frank's house, all within a little more than an hour. Yet she arrived to find two other guests' vehicles already in the driveway. Her heart sank a bit. She had imagined this might just be the two of them. Obviously the invitation was not a spur-of-the-moment one, but something Frank had planned. She wondered if her inclusion was an afterthought.

"Oh, well," she sighed, emerging from her vehicle. P.W.'s truck was a dead giveaway that he was one of tonight's entourage, but that other vehicle .... She studied the blue compact, then heard Jessica's voice wafting through a slightly ajar window at the front of the house.

"Just great," Harper mumbled, then checked

her attitude. *Breathe, relax, enjoy,* she instructed herself, by way of a quick pep-talk.

A chorus of lively barking heralded her arrival, and Frank popped his head out of the front door. "Harper!" he shouted. "Get in here before these wild animals make a break for it. I canna hold them off for long."

She smiled at his silly attempt at a brogue. He really was a nice man.

Inside, reintroductions were brief. Everyone oohed and ahhed over Harper's wine offering: a Cabernet Sauvignon from a popular Paso Robles winery.

"Let's save the good stuff to have with dinner," Frank said. He was already pulling the cork to let the wine breathe. "We've started with some pale ale from a local craft beer maker. Jessie picked it up."

For a second, Harper was confused. *Jessie? As in Officer Jessica Grady?* The familiarity caught her off guard.

"Harper?" Frank asked. "Can I interest you?"

"Ah, sure," she said, accepting a beer.

Once everyone was settled in the living room, Frank subtly nodded to Jessie and she took over.

"So, what Aza and you discovered is known as a 'trespass grow,'" she said, launching into her topic with authority.

"There are illegal marijuana plantations scattered throughout California state forests.

The U.S. Forest Service and law enforcement destroyed nearly a million marijuana plants from hundreds of sites statewide in 2013, and the numbers have continued to grow every year since. The Forest Service is going nuts because these farms are harming the trees and animal life.

"These growers divert water from streams for irrigation, leave tons of trash, and use large amounts of dangerous herbicides and pesticides. So, once we have the all-clear on evidence-gathering at this site, the service will be organizing a huge cleanup. They will be looking for volunteers from the community to help out." The group sat quietly for a minute, taking in the information.

Harper instinctively raised her hand. "What type of stuff needs to be hauled out?"

"Generally there's lots of hose for starters, then items like tents, sleeping bags, stoves, food, clothing," she said. "We've already swept for weapons and ammo and used metal detectors to find and snap the remaining traps. It's unlikely volunteers will find any stashes we missed."

"Sounds like you've dealt with this before," Harper said.

Jessie nodded. "We think the plantation is part of the work of a Mexican drug cartel operation in the area. We've got officers on this from the California Highway Patrol, the county sheriff's office, and even California Fish and Wildlife. This is not a local grow on private land for recreational use, or the type of small operation known as a mom-and-pop grow. So, we don't want to just destroy the plants, we want to catch the bad guys. Take care. You two stumbled onto a small part of something much larger."

Harper took a sip of her beer, which had grown warm.

"But why here?" she asked.

"The growers are looking for isolated sites with ample sun and water," Jessie said. "While Frank and Aza may use those old trails up beyond P.W.'s house, the public rarely ventures there. And most tourist traffic around here is just passing through on the way up to the lakes or ski areas. The growers probably thought they wouldn't be disturbed. The roads that lead out of that area from the other side of the mountain see very little traffic."

"What about the DNA testing on the evidence-hold dogs?" Harper asked. "How does that fit in?"

"Ah, the feces trail," Jessie said. "You never know what you'll find on a suspect's shoes or car mat. The DNA might help us place certain individuals as having been at the site of this trespass grow or another one."

P.W. gave Jessie a quizzical look. The deputy continued. "The testing is used a lot in planned communities and upscale apartment complexes to catch people who don't clean up after their animals," she said. "Canine excrement can be matched to a dog's DNA profile."

"And on that appetizing note," Frank said, "let me take the flank steak off the grill, and we'll get down to some serious eating."

They chose seats at the round dining table, leaving the one closest to the kitchen open for their host.

"Voila!" Frank said, producing a platter piled high with sliced meat. He joined them at the table and offered a simple grace. "For these and the many blessings received from thy bounty, O Lord, make us truly thankful. Amen."

"Amen," Harper echoed.

After the green salad and potatoes were passed, and the wine poured, Frank proposed a toast. "To new friends and old," he said, looking from Harper to Jessie.

Was it just Harper's imagination or did his gaze linger on Jessie? The woman looked good out of uniform. Her blonde locks were down and framed her heart-shaped face. Her black jeans managed to look both casual and sophisticated at the same time. Harper noticed a stain on the cuff of her own blouse. *I'm out of my league here,* she thought. And yet Harper imagined that once she got over her irrational feelings of jealousy toward the woman, perhaps the two of them could become friends.

"Where's Loretta tonight?" P.W. asked Jessica.

"A bit under the weather," she said.

"Ah," P.W. said. "Poor thing."

Great, Harper thought, *she's a dog person, too. No wonder Frank likes her.*

"And how's Sheldon doing?" Harper asked. After all, she liked dogs, too.

"Fair to middling, I suppose," P.W. said, "clomping around with a cast on his leg while the bones knit. The break doesn't seem to be bothering him too much, though."

A wide range of topics took up the dinner hour, and before long Frank was serving coffee and the chocolate cake that P.W. had supplied.

"That's gonna cost me a coupla extra miles on my run tomorrow," Jessie said, needling P.W. as she finished the last bite of her generous portion. Harper studied her own plate with its modest half-eaten serving. *Of course she runs,* Harper thought. *What doesn't she do?*

Jessie rose from the table. "Sorry to bail early, but I pulled the early weekender. I better be off and to bed."

P.W. also rose. "Yeah, I need to pick up Aza before he outstays his welcome over at Dania's house. That boy is gonna be asking for vegetarian meals if I let him eat over there too often. I trust you can help with the cleanup, Harper?"

Frank shot P.W. a look of slight annoyance, but the elder gentleman pretended not to notice. After goodbyes were said, Frank closed the front door and turned to Harper.

"You don't really have to stay and clean up," he said. "P.W.'s just a meddling old fool and fancies he's something of a matchmaker. Apparently, Aza takes right after him."

"No worries," Harper said, remembering that Aza had thought she was Frank's girlfriend. "And anyway, I'd like to help with the dinner dishes. It's early, and I've got nothing else going on." She immediately regretted her choice of words.

Frank gave her a wounded look, then grinned. "Wow. Dishes or nothing. Let's see if we can do better than that."

Once the last plate was wiped and put away, Frank proposed that they take the dogs out for last call. His foot wasn't ready for long hikes yet, but there was a wide, flat path to a nearby clearing where they could study the constellations while the dogs took care of business.

Harper hugged herself as they walked along in the chilly evening air. Viewed from the mountains, the stars were unlike any she had seen when she lived in metropolitan areas. The sparkling points seemed to form a canopy above their heads.

Frank suddenly jerked his arm upward. “There! A shooting star.” Harper threw her head back and caught sight of the tail as it extinguished.

“I always wonder if someone’s world was just snuffed away,” she said.

“Meteors,” Frank said. “A lot of them coming into earth’s atmosphere are visible from these mountains. The ones that aren’t meteors ... well, I wouldn’t worry too much about something millions of light years away that might not have had dire consequences.

“Whenever I study the night sky, it reminds me of something my father once said. ‘Up here there’s not much between you and God. You can see him pretty good.’” Harper laughed at the quote.

Frank started pointing out the constellations he could identify. Harper added a few of her own. When they were finally stumped, he called the dogs and they slowly headed back to the house.

Once inside Frank pulled his jacket off as Harper stood there shivering in hers. “I guess I should go,” she said with uncertainty.

Frank lightly grabbed her shoulders. “You don’t have to go yet, do you?” he asked, rubbing her upper arms. “I think I about froze you to death out there. I could light a fire and defrost you. Anyway, we haven't played any board games or endured nearly enough awkward silences."

Harper pursed her lips. "Okay, funny guy. I'll stay for one fire, maybe a board game and three awkward silences, but then I'm outta here."

Frank was true to his word. Soon a fire was roaring and the two were sitting on the floor playing a word game on the low coffee table. The dogs, Grin and Barrett, lounged on either side of the fireplace, just within petting reach. When the game was over, Frank poured ruby port into two small crystal glasses. They sipped by the firelight.

"You don't strike me as the fancy-glass type, Frank," Harper said, studying the etched pattern.

"A leftover from my days as a happily married man," he said. "I haven't had the heart to part with some things."

The words hung in the air, and Harper studied the flames.

"Of course, now that I think about it," he said, "I guess talking about one's dead wife is no way to impress a woman."

Harper turned her head to face him. "Is that what you're trying to do? Impress me?"

Her bluntness threw him. "You know," he said, "I really don't know what I'm doing. Just making it up as I go along, I guess."

Harper nodded, thinking: *Okay, this is the first awkward silence.*

"What about you and Jessie?" she asked.

Sheesh, where did that come from, she wondered as soon as the words were out of her mouth. *What's in this wine?*

Frank rubbed his hand over his jaw. "You are a perceptive one. I was hoping that didn't show. She's a great gal, and I do love her, but not in the way you are thinking."

Well, that's clear as mud, Harper thought. "Do you care to elaborate?"

Awkward silence No. 2 sat in the space between them. "Not at this time," Frank said. "Now let me help you up off this floor and onto the couch."

As they settled in on the sofa Harper thought Frank might put his arm around her shoulder, but he just pulled a throw quilt off the back of the couch to hand to her.

"Sorry the house is so cold. I don't use the heat much this time of year," he said. "Now where were we?"

"I was trying to figure out how it is that you are still single," Harper said, eager to pick up on the direction of her earlier questioning.

"You are a nosy ...." Frank stopped himself before he said woman. "Reporter. I bet you were good at your job."

"I was," Harper said, "and you are deflecting the question."

He stared into the fire. The flames were subsiding and the pieces of hardwood he had strategically placed in the grate were turning into embers. He'd have to get this part of the conversation over with.

"Simple story." He swallowed. "After my wife, Teresa, died, I couldn't imagine ever replacing her. She was the love of my life. When I did start playing the field, I compared every woman I dated to her, and they just didn't stack up. Or, more likely, my feelings for them didn't compare. I broke a lot of hearts until I realized what I was doing.

"When I met Jessie something in me opened back up. But that didn't work out, and it's been a long slow heal. I just don't know if I'm cut out to be part of a twosome anymore. Hell, I don't even know if I'd be a good date anymore. I've been single most of my life.

"As for Jessie, I'm not trying to be mysterious. We're great friends now. The rest of that story is just hers to tell, not mine."

Harper sat quietly and let the information sink in for a moment.

"Your turn," he said.

"Well," Harper said, "I was young and foolish when I married, and we didn't last. Did I mention I was blind too? Things never seemed to add up. Like where he was at all hours, why our bank account was so low, how come I couldn't seem to make him happy. Our marriage just sort of disintegrated.

"Now I see we were very different people. We shared some values, but not others. I think truth is important. He thought 'sparing my feelings' was more important.

"After the divorce, I threw myself into my career and never looked back. Journalists barely have time for lives, and dating within a newsroom has many pitfalls. In recent years, my folks fell ill. I juggled career and their care at first, then left my job completely." Harper spoke quickly, not wanting to dwell on her recent pain. "When they died, I decided to sell the family home and, with the money I'd come into, get a fresh start."

The last flame extinguished and embers glowed in the fireplace. Frank rose to stir the fire.

"Well, we're always happy to see another friendly face in St. Cross," he said. "I, for one, am glad you showed up here, Harper Henshaw. Not everyone would have thrown in with our eccentric ways, or accepted my old job at the animal shelter. I'm not sure how she did it, but I'd swear Edith Saint Cross selected you herself from the great beyond."

Harper laughed. Soon she was on the road

back home. They'd save awkward silence No. 3 for another day.

Frank stood by his front door a long time after he closed it, absentmindedly stroking the stubble on his chin. He had surprised himself by opening up to Harper about his personal history. Had he just set something in motion? He'd been down this road a few too many times since Teresa died. *So many women,* he thought, *so many mistakes.*

But this was the first time he had felt even a slight spark of interest in someone since he and Jessie broke up. If anything, he realized he had been intentionally keeping his contact with women to a minimum. Avoiding Harper didn't seem to be very practical.

Was he even attracted to her, or was he just ready to start dating again? Maybe it was the latter. Perhaps the time had come to reevaluate his single and abstinent status.

13

A call from Gene changed the course of Harper's week. He was on the line first thing Monday morning asking for a favor.

"Harper, I know you have a job there and other freelance assignments, but I could really use an on-site reporter on this. And it's right in your back yard."

"What have you got?"

"Grand old estate just came on the market there at a record price for the area. First time the mansion has been for sale in about 20 years. Agent can get you in for a tour. Earlier owners helped establish your new home town. Maybe you can stir up some local color. You ever heard of the Cross family?"

"Heard of them?" Harper said. "You can't live here and not stumble into their legacy on a daily basis. In fact, I know a man who I think grew up on the estate – the son of one of the family employees. I'll see if he'll come along on the tour with me. He'll probably have a few stories to tell."

"Great, Harper. Of course I needed it yesterday."

"You never did quite grasp the concept of a firm deadline did you Gene?"

"Oh, and Harper? Shoot some of your own photos to go with the canned stuff from the real estate agent. And maybe a video? Live tweets of the tour?"

"Go away, Gene. You'll get the story," Harper said. "And you're going to owe me. Remember this next time I submit a free-lance pitch. Great to hear from you. Bye now."

She moved to her desk and booted up her home computer. The keyboard had gotten dusty from disuse and lack of regular cleaning. Within minutes Harper had the real estate agent's number. She noticed he wasn't local, but from the San Francisco area. Maybe big money didn't deal with small-town real estate agents. He turned out to have enlisted the help of a local agent, and soon Harper was chatting with Melanie Span of Alta.

"Tomorrow?" Harper said. "Okay. Let me see if Mr. Simpson is available, and I'll confirm that. Probably mid-morning, say 10 a.m.?"

As she suspected, P.W. jumped at the chance to see the old place and agreed to be interviewed for the story. When she picked him up the next day she noticed he had dressed for the occasion. His slacks and shirt had sharp creases that spoke of recent ironing. He wore a tie, and had on a more casual jacket over the ensemble. Since he was a subject in her story, she studied him with an appraising eye.

The estate wasn't far out of town, only about a 10-minute drive from P.W.'s house. As they pulled in past the stone pillars that marked the gated entry to the property, he gave a low whistle. Harper stopped at the intercom to announce their arrival. Soon the ornate wrought-iron gates automatically pulled open to allow them to drive through.

"Well, we never had anything like that in my day," P.W. said. "Opened the gates by hand every morning and shut them up at night. Anyone needed our attention, they had to wait till morning or ring a bell by the gate and hope someone heard it. Otherwise they had to drive back to town and use the telephone."

The winding cobblestone driveway snaked up the wooded hillside. P.W. pointed out a small structure on the left that was attached to a car barn. "That was the gardener's apartment," he said. "The holding was near to 50 acres in those days. They'd keep a tractor there, other equipment and a spare automobile – in case the snow was too bad to get a vehicle down from the house."

Harper stopped the car and jotted down a few notes before continuing. As they passed through a second set of gates, this one sitting open, P.W. spied what he called "the caretaker's house" on the right. Three river-rock chimneys rose from the wood-shingled two-story.

"That's where we lived, but we weren't the only ones," he said. "You'd call that a triplex today. It was divided up for three families. The two maids shared the upstairs, and the cook had the basement studio. We were on the main floor. For the most part, staff needed to live here. The area was very remote in the 1920s when the main house was built. Back then the servant housing was in the attic."

"What did your father do, P.W.?" Harper asked.

"Oh you could say butler, but he managed the day-to-day running of the house," P.W. said. "Pop had a head for figures, so he kept the books for the groceries and other merchant purchases – supervised the staff. My mother handled the laundry, did the mending, things of that sort."

They passed through another set of gates that was also ajar. "Those are new, too," he said.

Harper wasn't quite sure what she'd been expecting, but based on the car barn and caretaker's house, she was prepared for a mountain-lodge-like mansion. Instead what greeted her was a kind of Beaux Arts Hearst Castle, albeit on a smaller scale and more squat than tall. She drove around the fountain at the center of the circular driveway and parked at the massive front door.

Harper turned off the ignition and grabbed her notebook and pen. Both she and P.W. tilted their heads to look up the gently rising stone stairs leading to the two-story foyer. The real estate agent had apparently been looking out through the leaded glass side panels and opened the front door as if on cue. The place had obviously been the site of a life of luxury in its day.

After introducing themselves to the agent, Melanie Span, they headed inside where Harper was amazed at how put together the place looked.

"The seller died more than a year and a half ago," Melanie said. "The estate auctioned off some of the furnishings but, for the most part, the rest are included in the list price of $7.9 million. Closer to San Francisco, a property such as this would easily be priced at five times as much."

P.W. proved to be a walking Cross-family history book. "That's the same old floor," he said, pointing at the wood parquet in the foyer. He waved his hand to eye level. "Those wall niches, too. That one displayed the family Bible, and the other, the Saint Cross family coat of arms."

"They had a family coat of arms?" Harper asked, scribbling as they walked.

P.W. chuckled. "I think a Cross family member had an artist make it up. Saint was his wife's maiden name. They used the combination of Saint Cross for all their offspring. Then, when the town was established, they named it St. Cross. Some early Western settlers didn't feel like they had much history, so there was a tendency to make some things sound a little grander than they were."

The real estate agent chimed in. "Yes, you can verify that at the library," Melanie said. "There's a family history on file."

P.W.'s eyes swept up to the chandelier. "Original," he said and moved onward into the room on the right. The agent's high heels clattered on the stone floors.

As they toured the ornate rooms, P.W. pointed out which pieces of furniture remained from the Cross family's days. Apparently there had been no market for a dining table that seated 20 when the estate of Edith Saint Cross sold, so the buyer had kept the heavy wooden piece.

"How did they even get that into this room?" Harper asked.

"Built it here," P.W. said. "Before my time, but that's the story I was always told. If you look at the size, there's no way to get the table out unless you were to cut it into pieces."

"What a trove of antiques," Harper said. Melanie handed her a property flyer and press release detailing the home's dimensions, current lot size of five acres and other statistics.

Next they entered the conservatory, a spacious corner room with two walls of windows and a grand piano. "This is where the choral society performed for decades," P.W. said. "Once a new owner is in place, there's some sort of rider to allow them to resume practicing here."

Melanie confirmed the fact. "The use is minimal compared to say, a life estate, where the new owner would have to let someone continue to live on the property," she said. "We don't anticipate this will present an obstacle to finding a buyer."

In the wood-paneled library, P.W. walked straight to the far wall and found the opening to a secret passageway. "Spent a lot of time playing in here as a child," he said. "The corridor leads to the speakeasy."

"Speakeasy?" Melanie asked.

"From Prohibition days," he said. P.W. clumped about six feet down the tight hall where he felt for a chest-high lever. "Had to stand on tiptoe to reach this in my day." After some jiggling, he was able to move a small pocket door aside and reveal a dark stairway.

"Here P.W.," Harper said. "Take my cellphone flashlight." Melanie also clicked hers on. The steep stairs opened to a basement level room overtaken by spider webs. Once their eyes adjusted to the dim light, they could see the room was furnished with a long wooden bar, antique-looking stools and some tables and chairs. The mirror behind the bar reflected their cell lights and revealed a line of half-empty booze bottles.

"Amazing," Harper said. "Melanie, do you think the late owner even knew this was here?"

"I have no clue," she said. "But I certainly had no idea. This room is not on the floorplan of the basement."

Once the threesome finished touring the other rooms, they headed to the back yard, where they were greeted by fresh air and sunlight. Behind the main house were gardens and a reflecting pool. Like the front fountain, it was empty. A late freeze would damage the aging water features if they were filled too soon.

Beyond the garage were stables and a riding ring. The three walked around the side of the house and returned to the front entrance, where Harper's car sat.

"I was wondering," P.W. said. "Would it be all right if we saw inside the caretaker's house?"

"The guesthouse?" asked the agent. "Well, we're not really showing it. I supposed I can let you in, but I'd prefer it not be part of your story, Harper."

"I can't guarantee that," she said. Then she thought of what it would mean to P.W. and softened her hard-nosed reporter stance. "Tell you what. I've got plenty here for my story. How about you just let P.W. take a look around? I can wait in the car."

And so it was that P.W. entered his childhood home alone. He closed the front door and took in a deep breath. He had expected that familiar smell – a mixture of supper cooking, freshly pressed clothes, and his mom's cat – but it was no more.

Unlike the main house, his old home was bare. The original kitchen had been ripped out and redone, as had the bathroom. His small bedroom had been converted into a closet/storage room. Whatever he had hoped to find wasn't there anymore. He looked out the back door onto the deck addition. That was newer, too.

Dust played in the sunlight coming in the east-facing window. There was nothing left of his folks or himself here. He returned to the car ready to head home to Aza and their life together.

14

Adam sat in the choir room office and checked his watch. He had time to review the Requiem before Mimi and the soloist candidates arrived. After last week's incident and short rehearsal, he would need to make up for lost time.

The director furiously jotted more notes in the margins of his well-worn score. Introit, rehearsal number 7: Requiem aeternam dona eis. "Treat this section as though it is a wondrous gift to the listener." Translation: Give them eternal rest, O Lord.

The Kyrie: Christ have mercy, Lord have mercy. "This is a plea that grows in volume and intensity, building to the double forte at rehearsal 17 and then subsiding into a piano at rehearsal 18."

He continued through the entire work, his

pencil flying, immersed in the music and the sounds he heard inside his head.

A knock on the door shook him from his reverie.

"Ah, Jim," Adam said, shuffling through his in-box for the audition lineup. "Come in. I think you beat Mimi here, but let's get you warmed up."

The lanky baritone, one of the college students joining them on the Duruflé, entered the room. Adam had him in a class and thought the young man showed some promise, although a career at the Met was not likely in the student's future.

Jim was a novice at auditions, and Adam seriously doubted the college freshman had loosened up his voice on the drive over. They'd need to use the time until Mimi's arrival by starting with a few warmup exercises. Adam began with having Jim hum a major scale up and then back down again. Mimi soon joined them, and the audition officially started.

"Now the baritone solos in Part III, the Domine Jesu Christe, and Part VIII, the Libera Me, can be sung by one soloist or split among two," Adam said. "Sometimes they are just sung by the choir, as the composer intended. This rather depends on the talent pool and how the parts suit a particular voice. Although we might not split them for a professional performance, we may for a church performance for, er...." The words he was thinking were "political reasons," but he decided against uttering the phrase. "Sometimes it's nice to spread these things out."

Adam droned on in a professorial tone. "And remember what you are singing about in both sections. In the Domine, you are begging that the dearly departed be spared the torments of hell. In the Libera Me, you pray they not be judged by fire and doomed to eternal death, but be delivered and rest in perpetual light."

After Jim worked his way through the parts, Harold Yukata showed up and ably ran through the solos. His older voice resonated with timbre, but his renditions lacked Jim's vitality. Adam thought of his revised budget, which had reduced the instrumentalists from a full orchestra to organ, strings, trumpet, harp, and timpani. There would be no paid soloists.

"Pity about the budget cutback," Adam said as Harold was getting ready to leave. "Your voice would lend itself so well to backing by an entire orchestra. We really can't give you the showcasing it deserves.

"I don't suppose there is some discretionary funding the church could throw our way? P.W. lacks any sort of understanding or experience in these matters. What right has Edith Saint Cross to put him in as chairman? The man has no finesse. You, on the other hand, have been on the board long enough to grasp the intricacies."

Harold, not known for being talkative, bobbed his head in weak agreement.

"I'm really not sure P.W. can even handle the position," Adam said, warming to his subject. "He's as old as the hills and, if I'm not mistaken, becoming quite forgetful. He could only run that meeting because Debbie and Frank told him what to do.

"You, on the other hand, have the experience and diplomacy to deal with delicate church situations. And you realize the importance of a vibrant music program to the life of this church and community.

"It's not like I'm suggesting a coup, but we are the stewards of this institution. I take that very seriously. And if P.W. is not up to the task, we must replace him ... for his own good and ours."

Harold considered Adam's viewpoint and nodded. He wasn't so much agreeing as letting Adam know he had heard what the director had said.

"Think about it, anyway. Let's keep an eye on P.W. He shouldn't be raising a young child, let alone running the church."

After a third baritone tried out, the sopranos started rolling in for the Pie Jesu solo. The more promising of the first two was the second, a college student named Gloria Vasquez.

"I'm looking for only a slight vibrato, which your young voice has," Adam said. "But I want you to feel a greater sense of tragedy. Make the tenors weep. And when you reach the high voice parts, you are at the emotional peak of the piece. Don't let your voice tighten here. Keep it supple and remember you are a mezzo."

Last up was Sammie.

"Okay, let's hear what you've got," Adam said. Based on what he had seen of her in rehearsal, he had little expectation that this audition would produce his soloist.

Sammie started shakily. She had hoped to run into Jim at the auditions – she really had no illusions of actually getting a solo. But only she, Adam, and Mimi were in the choir room.

The range of the solo, from a B flat at the low end up to an F sharp on the top, presented no difficulty for the teenager. But Sammie had little understanding of what she was singing about and wasn't paying attention to dynamics at all. She faltered on a few notes and misread some of the rhythms.

"Okay, that will do," Adam said as he gave her a cut off. "Thank you for your interest, Miss Hernandez. I think you might do some solo work one day, but you'll have to apply yourself. Take music courses and find a voice coach. Fortunately, I have a few minutes free now before I prepare for tonight's rehearsal so I can get you on your way. We'll start with scales." He turned his attention to his wife at the keyboard.

"Mimi, would you be a dear and trot down to the coffee shop to get me some caffeine," Adam asked. "You'll be sitting all evening. A walk will do you good."

After Mimi left, the director pulled the white board around and drew the parts of the throat for Sammie. Then he sat at the piano keyboard, and they ran scales for a few minutes. Sammie felt self-conscious singing in front of anyone, but at least she was singing in front of only one person. She found the act of creating music with her voice uncomfortably intimate.

Adam popped up from the piano bench. "You can actually manipulate the cartilage here at the front of your throat. The thyroid cartilage is held in place by ligaments, which are flexible. See how mine moves around?" He demonstrated. "Now you try."

Sammie hesitated, then gingerly touched her throat. Adam moved behind her. "May I?" he asked. She nodded yes.

He placed his finger on her throat gently rocking the protective covering back and forth. "Try again," he said. Sammie put her fingers on her throat. This time he placed his fingers over hers, guiding her movements. "Think of the exercise as a throat massage. I always include it when I'm warming up my own voice."

After a bit she stopped moving her hand, as did he. His fingers seemed to rest on hers an eternity and his body felt too close pressing along her back. She finally ducked away.

"Interesting," said Sammie, feigning an enthusiasm she did not feel. "Thanks for your time, but I just remembered something I need to do."

"Very well," Adam said, lost in his world of music and seemingly unaware of the teenager's discomfort. "Don't be late for rehearsal."

Sammie practically ran from the rehearsal room. She stopped to take a breath once she was outside. *Is it my imagination,* she wondered, *or is he a really creepy old guy?*

That night at rehearsal Adam took the choir through the entire Requiem, announcing the soloists along the way. Gloria Vasquez would have the mezzo part, while Jim Becker and Harold Yukata would split the baritone solos.

About midway through the evening, Frank's friend Hans from the Forest Service stopped in to announce the cleanup at the pot plantation site on Saturday and enlist volunteers to help in the effort.

Sammie could hardly wait for the second half of rehearsal to be over. She caught up with Jim on his way out the door. "Hey, Jim," she said. "Congratulations on your solo. You mentioned you'd like to see the animal shelter where I work. I'll be there Sunday afternoon until closing if you want to stop in."

"Thanks Sammie," he said. "Sorry I can't hang out. I bummed a ride over with one of the guys, and we've got a late-night study session for finals."

"Finals? Now?" she asked.

"Yeah, we're on a trimester system," Jim said. "Sorry. It's the finals grind. I gotta go."

"See you Saturday at the cleanup?" she asked.

"Sure thing," he said and pecked her on the cheek.

15

Saturday dawned clear and bright – it was a perfect day to be out in the woods. A small army of Forest Service workers seemed to have descended on the tiny village during the night. Two work crews in bright orange jumpsuits arrived from a correctional facility. Citizens of St. Cross and nearby communities gathered at the church in the first light to await transport up to the plantation site. A variety of off-road vehicles and ATVs – some official, many private – formed a line in the parking lot outside the St. Cross Church fellowship hall.

Inside, volunteers plied the workers with hot coffee, juice, and doughnuts. P.W. handed out bottles of water.

"Make sure to take at least two," he said. "There will be more water up at the site. Lunch will be available both on the mountain and down at the church."

Aza and other children who had tagged along with their parents played on the equipment in the St. Cross Preschool yard.

Harper was impressed by the level of community involvement and fast mobilization of resources. She waved at Frank through the crowd and fell into line to board a vehicle behind Debbie Benes and Harold Yukata. The board members were huddled together with heads close, whispering intensely. They didn't notice her.

"That's ridiculous," Debbie said through clenched teeth. "Of course he's suitable to be chairman, and he's done a fine job parenting. He just has his own style."

Harper tried to keep her distance, but she eavesdropped.

"But his memory," Harold said. "His carelessness is likely responsible for the vandalism at the church. And that drug dealers may have come into his house to steal keys? You can't say that's safe for Aza."

"You don't know carelessness has anything to do with this." Debbie spat out her words. "And we don't know if drug dealers were at the church or his house. Don't borrow trouble where none exists."

The driver of a dusty navy-blue van called another six people forward, and the two terminated their conversation. Harper frowned and dropped back to await the next vehicle.

The ride up the mountain was longer than Harper had imagined. Had she really walked this far in bad weather? The snow was gone, except under some of the fuller pines and in deep hollows where it had accumulated during the long winter.

Harper marveled at how beautiful the surroundings were. She hadn't left town since the ill-fated mountain adventure in search of Aza. She would have to get outside more.

They passed several Forest Service crews removing irrigation hoses. Black plastic bags bulged with refuse. Harper recognized Hans and waved at him.

Her vehicle stopped at what appeared to be the main encampment. The volunteers would be cleaning out tents and other makeshift structures before they were taken down.

Harper spotted Sammie in what had been the mess hall of sorts. "Thank god," Sammie said. "I can use a hand with this. I'm sorting out whatever food can be donated and then trashing the rest."

A pile of boxes stood at the ready, as did a roll of bags.

"Box the food we're keeping. Bag the items that are opened or expired," Sammie said. "This will be a gold mine for the food pantry."

"I didn't know there was a food pantry," Harper said. She thought she knew St. Cross pretty well after her first few months in town, but apparently there was more to be discovered.

"At the back of Neal's General Store," Sammie said. "It's called the Senior Food Pantry, but anyone can get food there. I wonder if they even have room to store all this."

"Let me guess," Harper said. "Another creation of Edith Saint Cross?"

"No, actually, Neal's bought out the previous grocer and all his stock, but I guess some of the stuff was pretty gross," Sammie said. "Like the kind of processed foods that were popular in the '70s. So he moved that to the back to give away and restocked the front with more healthy choices and organic stuff."

Harper made a mental note to try shopping at the general store instead of driving to the chain grocery in Riverdale. She thought it was important to support local businesses when she could – especially in such a small town.

Before long, a group of college students disembarked from an SUV, and Jim Becker joined them inside the mess tent.

"Hey, Sammie," he said, seeming genuinely pleased to see the teenager. "I was worried it would be hard to find you. Can I give you a hand?"

"Sure thing," she said. "Move these cases of Spam onto the food-bank pile."

Harper thought she would leave the young people to their work and headed out, trash bags in hand, to clean out some of the sleeping tents.

A volunteer holding a clipboard gave her instructions. "You work on these three tents and report back when they are cleared and can be taken down," he said. "We aren't salvaging clothes or sleeping bags, anything that could be soiled or contaminated in any way. We will take lanterns, cook stoves, flashlights, and items along those lines that can be cleaned up and resold at the thrift shop."

Harper felt claustrophobic inside the first green tent. She donned her work gloves and shoved shoes, dirty socks, underwear, and T-shirts into her bags along with cigarettes, trash, and random rolls of toilet paper. She was surprised to find feminine products. Harper had wrongly assumed a pot-growing operation would exclusively hire men.

What a waste, she thought, tying the garbage bag shut. She was amazed at her own ignorance about what was happening on state forestlands.

In the next tent Harper came along a stash of family-type photos. She pulled a small white bag from her jeans. Potential evidence was to be bagged separately. Outside she could hear two men talking. They were dismantling tents that had already been cleared.

"Yes, I've heard that these grows can be as large as 40,000 plants," said one of the men, who had a slight East Indian accent. Harper recognized the voice as that of Kevin Cheema, the real estate agent who had found her the bungalow she bought and who served on the church's board of directors. "They come in, clear the land, divert the streams, and kill off the small-animal population with rodenticides."

"That's true," said his companion. "And did you see all the deer carcasses back in the dump area? These guys don't even eat what they kill. Just shoot them and leave them to rot when the animals bother their crop.

"Hey, by the way," he said, "what happened to the front door at your church? I drove by and noticed it's boarded up. You guys closing up?"

"Not likely," Kevin said. "I suspect vandalism. Might be related to the drug activity in our area, but my money is on teenagers. We've got some young people singing with us for the upcoming Requiem. They have access to the building more than most. You're a teacher at the high school. Do you know anything about this Samantha Hernandez?"

"Sammie? Sure. Reserved. Polite enough. Never caused any trouble that I know about. Why?"

An approaching helicopter drowned out the remainder of the conversation. Choppers would be moving in and out all day, hauling large nets filled with garbage and irrigation hose.

Harper dragged bags of trash out of the tents she had cleared and over to the collection area that Mr. Clipboard had indicated. She was sweating from being inside and took a long drink of her water. The midmorning sunshine was heating up the pine forest, releasing the trees' characteristic scent. She closed her eyes and drew in the fresh smell. The fragrance was far preferable to the odor in the tents, which reminded her of a high school locker-room.

An air horn squawked at noon, and volunteers drifted to the drop-off area to collect bag lunches. Others boarded vehicles to head back to the church and eat lunch there before heading off to parts unknown. A line formed at the portable toilets.

Those who stayed on the mountain found stone overhangs or tree-shaded spots to eat their midday meals. Harper discovered a boulder with both shade and a view. She settled in to enjoy the break. After eating, she lay back on the rock and almost drifted off to sleep. An incoming helicopter signaled that lunchtime was over.

As the afternoon wore on and the temperature rose, exhausted volunteers headed down the mountain. Some chose to go on foot, but the bulk waited for rides. The vehicles returned with new supplies of ice-cold drinking water.

Harper was amazed at the number of people she talked to who had been on this type of cleanup before. Several gave her their phone numbers. She planned on doing follow-up interviews for her story. She found the magnitude of the problem of pot farms on state land staggering, and she imagined the scene playing out over and over again throughout the year. Finally, sunburned and exhausted, she hitched a ride down the mountain.

In the church yard, young Aza had appointed himself official greeter of people exiting the vehicles. His formality amused Harper.

"You can wash up over there, ma'am," he said, pointing to a makeshift setup. "Or if you need to use the bathroom, head around back to the potties. Then come inside the fellowship hall for something to eat."

"Thank you," she said. He peered up at her.

"Hey, I know you! It's Harper. Hey, everybody, here's the lady who saved Sheldon and Frank!"

Harper reached out to touch the top of his head. He stepped away.

"Wow," Aza said, "you're really dirty."

"Thanks for noticing, buddy," Harper said. "I'll take you up on that offer of something to eat as soon as I've washed off some of this crud."

She heard P.W.'s voice from behind her. "Now let the lady get on about her business.

Who made you the hygiene police? You're supposed to be bringing the volunteers in for something to eat, not scaring them away."

Harper turned to face P.W. "This operation is amazing," she said. "How did you pull this off?"

"With office comes privilege," he said. "Local residents, merchants and charities donated some things. Then I just did what I always have: asked my old friend Edith Saint Cross for a little help. Tapped the church discretionary spending for some funds and got her lawyers to cough up from the general emergency monies she set aside for the rest.

"As for the victuals, Neal's decided it was time to clear out the food pantry to make way for the new stock. It's made for some pretty, er, unusual dishes. I'd steer clear of the fisherman's stew if I were you."

"I'll keep that in mind," Harper said. "Thanks."

"Think nothing of it," P.W. said. "All part of my duties as board chairman."

"Well, if this is any indication, you're doing an admirable job," Harper said, and headed off to wash.

16

Services seemed to come a bit too early for most of the St. Cross Church parishioners on this particular Sunday. More than half the congregation had put in a full day at the Saturday cleanup.

Light streamed through the intact half of the stained-glass double doors. The broken panel had been removed for repairs and replaced with unsightly plywood.

The morning sun also shone through the arched windows along one side of the sanctuary, causing churchgoers to adopt a somewhat unorthodox parishoners arrangement. Two rows would be full, then two mostly empty, the pattern repeating itself three times. Most weeks the choir outnumbered those sitting in the pews.

After the organ prelude, Debbie Benes moved to the front to give the welcome and make announcements. "We can use some volunteers to help restock the food pantry. Anyone who is able should meet at 1 p.m. behind the general store. But first, the entire congregation is invited to lunch in the fellowship hall. There are leftovers from yesterday. Afterwards, you can head over to the food pantry or stick around to help clean up, as well as box and freeze any remaining food."

A Call to Worship followed, along with an opening hymn and the Prayer of Confession. Before long, Pastor Bryce Conroy ascended the pulpit to preach on the Israelites' journey through the desert. He recalled Operation Save Our Sierra, a 2009 effort in which $1 billion worth of marijuana was seized in Fresno County. "Perhaps this is our journey through the desert," he said, tying the ancient text to modern circumstances.

At the end of worship, Harper waited in line to shake Pastor Conroy's hand. As she neared him, she held back a bit. The reverend seemed to be having a rather spirited conversation with one of the regular churchgoers.

"But don't you just make the check out for the same amount each week?" Pastor Conroy asked.

"No," came the response. "I usually make

out the check based on how good the sermon was. And in your case, I'll probably be taking money out of the plate."

Harper decided to step out of line and greet the reverend another day. Remembering P.W.'s admonition about the fisherman's stew, she headed home to grab a salad and change into more casual clothes. She had several hours of shelter paperwork ahead. Following the busy physical weekend, she was ready for some solitude and sitting.

Her afternoon turned out to be quite illuminating. As she pored over shelter records, she found that Frank had devised an extensive foster system among the town residents. As opposed to outright adoptions, in which the new owners took on all responsibility for an animal, fosters received compensation for food and veterinary care for the animals they took into their homes. No doubt the arrangement was funded by Edith Saint Cross.

Curious about the high number of what he labeled "permanent fosters," Harper went online and started looking up the foster residents by name in a voters' registry database. She retained access to a few reporter research tools. Many were age 65 and older. In a work-around of sorts, Frank appeared to have been placing the bulk of the animals with the elderly.

She opened another notebook labeled "Call List." Here Frank had dutifully listed telephone calls he had made around town, seeking permanent homes for shelter pets. Dates, phone numbers, whom he spoke with, family size, and other information was included. The notes portion was extremely helpful: Not at this time. Try back next year. Resident will only accept poodles or non-allergenic varieties. Cats only.

Next she scanned the "Adoptions" book. Looking back well over a year she found a familiar name. Aza Simpson. Dog: Sheldon. Fees paid: $36.

The job was actually much more involved than Harper had imagined. Her role would be that of animal promoter, as well as manager of the day-to-day operations of the facility. She spied the stack of bids for her foundation work sitting on the counter. *Yes,* she thought, *this is the right thing to do on so many levels.*

The phone rang.

"Frank," Harper said. "Speak of the devil."

"What did I do now?"

"Just going over the shelter files," she said. "This is quite the system you have in place."

"Well, you needn't follow it to the letter, but the system works," Frank said. "Listen. I wanted to ask you over to my place Friday for a party. I mean a real party, not a dinner party. I'm inviting about 20 or so. It occurred to me that I know a lot of people in our age range that you might want to meet. Help you settle into St. Cross faster."

"Frank, that's a lovely idea," Harper said, touched by the gesture. "I'll be there. Can I bring any food?"

"Just something you'd like to drink if it's other than beer," he said. "I've got the eats figured out."

"Shall I come over early and help you get ready?"

"Sure, if you like. Come by around 6:30. That'd be great."

17

Early Monday Frank was back at church, making sure that the new locks were all functioning well and that cleanup efforts from the weekend events were completed, or nearly so. The rental company stopped by to pick up the portable toilets, but for the most part the parish grounds were quiet.

He puttered his way through the fellowship hall, stacking errant chairs and wiping down a few grimy windows. Then he sorted through the kitchen, put washed pots away, and saw what was left in the church refrigerator and freezer. Some decent food remained. He placed a quick call to the head of the deacons. He got a machine.

"Hey, Lydia, can you work your magic on the phone tree?" he asked. "There's food at the church that can be delivered to some of the house-bound locals. Thanks."

On a whim he decided to get a bit of fresh air and headed over to the graveyard that sat at the far end of the property. He hadn't paid his respects for quite some time.

Frank stopped first at the stone marking Edith Saint Cross' resting place. The marker sat in deep shade, and the last remnants of icy snow clung to the ground around it. The fence behind the granite slab needed repair, he noted. That was another chore to place on his never-ending list. He was somewhat surprised that P.W. hadn't tended to Edith's grave better. Frank studied the lettering of her name and the years she had lived. The tombstone was quite plain, really, for a woman of her wealth.

He walked to the opposite end of the yard and bowed his head at a simple marker reading: Teresa O'Brien. He liked the sunny spot and had bought the plot next to hers in a moment of grief. Since then he'd decided that the whole practice of burying corpses was somewhat morbid. "Just burn me up and plant me under some pines," he whispered. Maybe one day he'd place P.W. here instead.

Frank sometimes wondered if Teresa knew what he was doing, how he was aging, when he visited her grave. He hoped there was a heaven, some great beyond, but he didn't dwell on that much. There was enough to deal with here on Earth.

After Teresa died, both her folks passed on. Frank lost contact with her cousins, who had sent Christmas cards those first few years. He had moved on with his life. Since he was on site almost daily, however, he'd spruce up the graveyard and make sure the gardeners didn't neglect the grounds.

As Frank was turning from Teresa's grave, he heard cars pulling into the gravel parking lot. *Awfully early for anything to be going on here,* he mused. Monday was a non-staff day for the most part. The church offices were closed.

He looked up just in time to see Adam heading inside. He didn't place the others at first, but then realized they were members of the personnel committee. In fact, there were just enough of them to make him think there was a meeting. Once again it struck him that Monday morning seemed like a strange time to be conducting business, unless there was another emergency. But where was P.W.? And where was the personnel committee head, Debbie?

Something was going on, and Frank didn't like the looks of it. A knot began forming in his stomach. He thought back to several years earlier, when church members had tried to replace the longtime secretary and failed.

A shiny new sports car pulled into the visitor's

lot. Frank recognized the woman who emerged as Patricia Grayson, a partner with the law firm of Grayson & Sleigh, which handled Cross estate affairs. He pulled his phone from his pocket and rang Debbie. Her voice mail answered. "Debbie, if you're around, high-tail it over to the church ASAP. Patricia Grayson is here with most of the personnel committee. I don't see P.W. Whatever is going on can't be good."

Since he had handed over the chairman reins, Frank didn't have an official capacity on the board, although he expected to be called from time to time to offer maintenance and site-usage reports. Nevertheless, he planned to insert himself into the current proceedings – whatever they were. Putting on a stern expression, he waltzed into the conference room as though he owned the place.

"Mr. O'Brien, we weren't expecting you," Adam said, his usually confident voice cracking. Frank cut him off and greeted the assembled. "Ms. Grayson, Adam, Harold, Mrs. Carey, Kevin, Julia, Rodrigo. How nice to see you all. Don't let me hold things up. We wouldn't want Ms. Grayson's billable hours to eat too deeply into the church treasury."

Adam called his bluff. "Frank, this has nothing to do with you. This is a closed meeting of the personnel committee. Leave."

"Last time I checked, *you* weren't on the

personnel committee, either," Frank said. "You leave."

"But I am a material witness and have a vested interest in the outcome here," Adam said. "My programs are the ones suffering because of P.W.'s malfeasance."

"Malfeasance?" Frank nearly shouted.

"Gentlemen," Patricia said with authority. "If I had a gavel, I would rap it. Be quiet, both of you, if you want to stay. There's nothing in the operating documents preventing you or even P.W. from attending this ad hoc committee meeting. You just can't vote, should it come to that."

Frank was becoming concerned. Did the music director intend to oust P.W. or lay some sort of blame on him? Adam had seemed on edge since the stained-glass door was vandalized. Was this what he had been dreaming up?

"But Debbie, the committee chairperson, isn't here," Frank said.

"She was unavailable," Patricia said. "My office has been contacted regarding the current running of the board of directors of St. Cross Church. At question is the mental competency of the chairman of the board, Phinehas Simpson."

"What?" Frank yelled this time. "Mental competency?"

"Mr. O'Brien, please," Patricia said, levelling

a stare at him. "If you can't contain yourself, you will be asked to leave.

"As you all know, Mr. Simpson and Edith Saint Cross were lifelong friends. His appointment was at her behest," she said. "Grayson & Sleigh and our representatives do have the authority to overturn codicils to her will if circumstances meet certain standards."

Patricia turned to face Adam. "Age is not such a circumstance, Mr. Frasier. In fact it would be discriminatory and in violation of the law. We have no authority to order a competency hearing for Mr. Frasier based on no evidence, regarding his performance of a position he has held for only a short while. A review of the books since he took office shows no misspent funds or other irregularities."

"But the man is losing it," Adam said. "He's barely competent to raise a child, let alone run a church."

Patricia's face froze. "We are aware that he is the guardian of a minor child. A court of law appointed him and keeps tabs on their arrangement. You cannot be suggesting that the court is in error. As for the church, the issue of Mr. Simpson's competency is irrelevant.

"The operating documents clearly state that should any criminal activity take place on church property, the board may be suspended and a conservatorship appointed while a formal review is conducted. Until the sheriff determines whether the recent vandalism was in fact related to drug trafficking occurring on the premises, this board is on probationary status. Staff remains in place – for now.

"Thank you for calling your concerns to our attention, Mr. Frasier," she said, rising to leave. "Our management company will be dropping by periodically to keep tabs on the situation and your performance, Mr. O'Brien. Good day."

Patricia's dress shoes clicked along the wooden floor, and the door shut behind her with a clank.

Frank fought a strong urge to dive across the table for Adam's neck. Wrestling with his self-control, he stormed out of the room.

18

Frank went straight from the church conference room to his truck and slammed the door.

This is bad, he thought, *really bad. That bastard is not only trying to move P.W. aside at the church, but he is questioning the man's ability to care for Aza. Worst-case scenario, I'll have them both move in with me. No one is separating that boy from P.W.*

Frank started his vehicle, intending to head straight to P.W.'s house, but realized he was nearly out of gas. When he stopped to fill up, he remembered to check his phone. Debbie had texted him back. "What on earth are you doing at church this hour on a Monday morning? This is supposed to be the caretaker's day off. I'm with P.W. at the Coffee Klatch. Come join us."

Frank couldn't remember when he'd been this upset. Even in the forest with a bum foot and lame dog, he had felt the situation was under control at all times. Well, most of the time. This, however, seemed to be rapidly spinning out of his sway. How could he break the news to P.W.?

Just to complicate matters, as Frank pulled into the local restaurant's parking lot he noticed Patricia Grayson's sports car. *Just great,* he thought. *What are the chances she'd stop off for breakfast?*

Frank hurried into the restaurant as fast as his mending foot would allow. He saw P.W. wave from a booth in the back. To his surprise, Patricia was sitting next to P.W.

The old man was laughing heartily and shaking his head from side to side as Frank slid in beside Debbie.

"I'm so sorry," P.W. said, tears forming at the corner of his eyes. "We had no idea you'd turn up for that performance. But from what Patricia is telling me, you actually made the whole scene more believable."

Confused, Frank was at a loss for words.

"I'm sorry, too," Debbie said. "We set the meeting so early, on a Monday, assuming no one else would be around. Imagine my shock when you tried to summon me 'ASAP.' When you asked me to 'hightail' it over there, I thought I was in a western movie."

P.W. and Debbie burst into laughter in unison. She dabbed at her eyes with her napkin. Apparently they'd been laughing for a few minutes.

Frank raised his hands. "Okay. Uncle. What the hell is going on?"

P.W. and Debbie dissolved into another round of giggles.

"May I?" Patricia asked. Obviously Debbie and P.W. were too broken up to put Frank out of his misery.

"Adam contacted my office with his concerns after the vandalism. Then, when I ran into Debbie in Alta, she mentioned that he had taken Harold aside to discuss P.W.'s possible inability to handle the chairman position. I was not concerned about his competency. The chairman role is rather perfunctory. Other than an individual's ability to influence thinking, there is no real power.

"Knowing how insidious church politics can be, Debbie and I concocted this little plan to nip the matter in the bud, so to speak. Harold helped us set it in motion," she said. "You were never supposed to stumble upon the clandestine meeting."

P.W. and Debbie were having trouble containing themselves. "You leave," Debbie said, pretending to shout at P.W. and jutting out her jaw.

"No, you leave," P.W. replied in jest, his gnarled finger jabbing at the air between them.

Frank sighed and shook his head. "I see you've given these clowns the blow-by-blow."

Patricia smiled. "That was some of the best entertainment we've had in St. Cross for a while."

"Malfeasance?" P.W. said.

"Now, don't make me rap my gavel," Patricia replied.

"Holy shit," Frank said, dropping his head into his hands. "Enough. Get me some coffee and a menu."

"Oh, and the probationary status?" Patricia said. "Just made that up on the spot. Got a bit off-script when your unscheduled arrival changed the dynamics."

Patricia finished her coffee and excused herself. She had clients to meet.

P.W. had regained some of his composure.

"Frankie," he said, earnestly. "That temper of yours is gonna get you in real trouble one day. I can take care of myself. But shouting at people in a church meeting? Swearing around ladies? Your mama raised you better than that."

"I came close to doing worse," Frank said. "After Patricia left I almost launched myself across the table for Adam's throat."

That did it. Debbie and P.W. were consumed by another fit of laughter.

19

The next day Jessica Grady pulled her black-and-white into the Frasiers' paved driveway. Only one car – a red compact – sat outside. The deputy was hoping to get the fingerprint results soon, but in the meantime she wanted to check a few things in her report of the church vandalism incident.

Her knock on the front door of the white clapboard house did not produce Adam. His wife, Mimi, stood before her. "Mrs. Frasier? Do you mind if I come in? I've got some questions I'd like to ask you and Adam."

As Mimi stepped aside to let Jessica pass, her expression turned grim. *What fresh hell is this,* she wondered. "I'm sorry. Adam is out."

Without giving Mimi any information, the deputy asked if it was possible that Adam had touched the bell before she arrived on the scene last Thursday. Mimi was not very helpful.

"Well, he might have," she said. "You see I stayed back in case there was any danger. Adam was, of course, concerned for my safety."

Jessica studied her notebook. "Well, you told me at the time that you entered together."

Mimi's eyes flickered slightly. "Yes, I suppose I did," she said. "I was very unnerved by the whole affair."

Mimi immediately regretted her choice of words. Jessica was an astute cop and picked up the subtle shift in the atmosphere between them.

"Mrs. Frasier," she said, "this is a law enforcement investigation that may have ties to organized crime. If you are withholding any information, you may come to regret it."

Mimi straightened and looked Jessica in the eye. "I assure you, Deputy Grady, I have nothing else to offer on this matter."

Jessie closed her notebook. "Tell Adam, he'll need to come 'round the station. I have some more questions for him, too."

After Mimi closed the front door, she sank into her reading chair and opened her Bible to Corinthians 13. She started verse 4, then skipped on to verse 7. "Love ... always protects, always trusts, always hopes, always perseveres." She hadn't told everything she had seen. How could she defend lying to law enforcement?

The fingerprint matches from the church hand bell came in Wednesday morning. Jessie sat at the utilitarian desk in her spartan office, studying the report. A skim was forming on a lukewarm cup of what had passed for coffee with cream when the beverage was hot.

Technicians had found likely matches for two sets of prints. One set appeared to be Adam's, and the other belonged to a convicted shoplifter they had identified through their database.

Adam's prints were larger and partially blocking out the shoplifter's set, meaning that he appeared to have last handled the bell. The sheriff's deputy planned to put the fear of God in Adam Frasier and have him come in for a talk.

Jessie was not one to play cat-and-mouse. She preferred just to pounce. Although she could come up with no motive for Adam to throw the bell through the front door, his story wasn't adding up. How had his prints gotten on the bell when he said he hadn't touched it? And she had left his house yesterday certain that Mimi knew more than she was telling.

The deputy had sent a car to the couple's house to escort Adam in for questioning. Truth be told, the cops were just on a routine run into

St. Cross as part of their rounds, but Adam wouldn't know that. He'd think they were sent straight from hell just for him.

Guessing how important appearances were to the music director, Jessie thought that a cruiser tailing him into the station would bug him no end. *Let the mind games begin,* Jessie thought.

Adam's booming voice carried from the reception area. "Of all the indignities. I know my way to the sheriff's station."

The intercom clicked in her office. "Mr. Frasier is ready for interviewing, ma'am," came the disembodied voice.

"Room One," she said. "Be there in a minute."

When she entered the largely barren room, a very agitated Adam was seated in a straight-back chair on one side of the table. Jessie shot the accompanying deputy a questioning glance.

"He gave us some trouble, ma'am," the young officer said.

"I did not," Adam said, obviously perturbed. "Am I going to have to call my attorney?"

Jessie stopped him by putting her flat palm up in his direction.

"Thank you, deputy," she said. "Adam, we're just going to have a friendly chat here about church business."

The assisting officer stood at rest against the wall in the back of the room while Jessie settled in across the table from Adam. She got straight to the point.

"Cecelia Washburn," Jessie said, watching Adam's face for a reaction. He blanched. She controlled her face so the corners of her lips wouldn't turn up in a smile.

"Now, do you really want your attorney here? We're not charging you with anything just yet. I'm simply following up on a line of inquiry in a drug-trafficking investigation."

The surprised look on Adam's face turned to puzzlement. "What?"

Since Jessie had his attention, she would pursue her questions. She had no intention of answering his.

"There are two sets of prints on the hand bell we retrieved from the church vandalism incident," Jessica said. "Debbie Benes, who happens to play that bell, said she always wears gloves. The findings support her statement. We did not lift any of her prints. But we *did* identify yours and a set belonging to one Cecelia Washburn. As luck would have it, she's in our system."

"How would I know anything about this Cecelia person? I may have touched the bell without thinking when Mimi and I came into the church. I don't remember."

"Why don't you start by telling me how you know Cecelia," Jessie said. Adam sat without answering. "Your prints are over hers in several spots. Obviously, you handled that bell after she did. I want to know why."

Adam maintained his silence.

"Okay. The other possibility is that you threw the bell. Now which is it?"

Jessie stared him down. Finally Adam let out a heavy sigh.

"I didn't even know her last name," he said, looking at the floor. "We had a brief, ah, friendship, and she must have lifted the bell once when she was at the church. When I tried to break off the friendship with her, she got angry and returned the bell with a note attached. I must have touched the bell as I retrieved the note. Cecelia indicated she was planning on blackmailing me."

Jessie allowed herself a half-smile and tilted her head to the side just a bit. "Now that wasn't so hard, was it?" she said. "Do you still have the note?"

"No."

"You are free to go," she said, rising to leave. "Just pray that your stories line up. I know where to find you if I need you."

"Is she in custody? Is this related to the drug trafficking?" Adam asked. "Do you seriously think she is involved in that?"

"I'm not free to divulge any information at this time," Jessie said. She doubted Adam's extracurricular activities had any bearing on the trespass plantation inquiry.

"But what about the blackmail?"

"Until and unless your 'friend' actually does start to blackmail you, it's just a threat," she said. "Besides, we have no evidence. You said yourself that you no longer have the letter."

Adam hesitated, as though he might have more to say, then he stormed out of the sheriff's station.

Angry and shaken, the choir director went straight to his small office off the church rehearsal room. His encounter with the sheriff's deputies had unnerved him.

He sat in the tiny room and held his head. *That bitch Cecelia is nothing more than a criminal,* he thought, *and a kleptomaniac of sorts, no doubt.* How had he been so blind to her baseness? She had seemed so special – a bright light shining on his everyday humdrum existence, a bit of excitement – and yet it turned out she was common.

What compulsion had driven him to seek out the Cecelia Washburns of the world throughout his 12-year marriage, he wondered. He could do better, and he had done better with Mimi. She was his true love. A perfect rose to be set on a pedestal. So, why was he in his current predicament?

Mimi looked up to him, praised him, and complimented his accomplishments. Why wasn't that enough? The weight of guilt settled around his shoulders.

Adam shook himself from his thoughts and texted Mimi to say he would be home that night for dinner. He picked the phone up again and tapped in "My love."

His mind returned to Cecelia. "Bitch," he muttered, just as Pastor Conroy popped his head into the music director's office.

"And hello to you too, Adam," said the reverend, his face concerned. "Caught you in a weak moment, have I? Anything you'd like to tell me about?"

"Sorry, fa – reverend," replied Adam, who was raised Catholic. "Or is it minister? I can never keep track of the denominations."

"I'm Methodist, actually, and I respond to just about anything. But mostly to Bryce. I'm preaching this Sunday and didn't the find the music offerings in my box."

From his in-box Adam pulled a sheet detailing the hymn and anthem selections, and he handed it to the minister.

"You know," Bryce said, "this could be the reason God invented email."

Adam raised his hands in mock supplication. "I know, I know. But tell that to our aged church secretary."

Bryce nodded and with a "Thank you, kind sir" was off.

By the time Adam arrived at his front door he was feeling more settled. This time there was no black-and-white in the driveway to escort him away. *This will all work out.*

He stepped inside, closing the chill behind him. As he turned to let the warmth of the room envelope him he was met instead with hot fury. Mimi was on him, pounding his chest with her balled up fists.

"What was on that piece of paper you found wrapped around the hand bell?" she demanded. "Why did you pocket it? Why didn't you give it to the deputy? What is wrong with you?"

She stepped back. She wanted answers.

Adam looked like a man caught with his pants down. Realization dawned as the look on his face confirmed her suspicions.

"Not again," she said. "Not another affair!"

He stood perfectly still, his head bowed and eyes downcast. Mimi flailed at his chest once again with her slender hands, before she thought better of it. He was not worth the wasted motion. She headed upstairs to lock herself in their bedroom.

Adam felt as though his legs would give

way before he reached the liquor cabinet. What had he been thinking – meeting Cecelia at the church for a tryst? But driving to an outlying town to a cheap hotel would have eaten into their time together. Plus, he couldn't hide the expense from Mimi. And there was always the chance he would be seen. At the church he could drop in at odd hours, and his wife would assume he was working – perhaps with a soloist or voice student.

Then Cecelia decided she wanted more than a lover. She started showing up at hours she knew he would be there working. Once she dropped in unexpectedly before a Thursday night choir practice and started a row, slamming a stack of hymnals onto the floor before stalking out. Adam had been straightening up when Frank O'Brien arrived. They had come very close to being discovered.

The next week Cecelia made her intentions clear. She wanted Adam to leave Mimi. And if she couldn't have that, she wanted money to go away. Another argument ensued. Before he knew what Cecelia was doing, she had pulled a bell case from the shelf and emptied the contents. Only later did he realize that she had pocketed one of the bells in the process. Then Cecelia "returned" the bell wrapped in a threatening letter.

Adam grabbed a crystal tumbler and poured

himself a Scotch. Then he sat down heavily on the brown leather couch. Flicking on the side table lamp, he removed the crumpled note from where he had hidden it in the back of a Renaissance music tome. He scanned the handwritten letter. *What damage is there left for her to do,* he thought. Mimi already knows, and so does law enforcement.

But then he considered his jobs. Directing the choir wasn't his main source of income, but he couldn't afford to lose the position or have word get around the Sierra Foothills campus where he worked on the faculty. He had lost too many other jobs, and the expense of frequent moves had eaten into the Frasiers' meager bank accounts.

He downed the rest of his drink. *Maybe Cecelia is bluffing,* Adam thought. *Maybe she'll only "tell" Mimi.* That Mimi knew about the note anyway and had guessed his infidelity was a fluke, but did put that worry to rest.

Perhaps emboldened by the booze, Adam made a decision. He would not fold to blackmail. Mimi would eventually forgive him. She always did.

None of this was really his fault anyway, he rationalized. Eve had caused the Fall in the garden. Cecelia was a temptress who had seduced him. His feet might be made of clay, but the rest of him was made of stronger stuff.

He poured a second Scotch and sipped this one, feeling more confident in himself. No woman was getting the better of him.

20

By the time Thursday evening rolled around and the Frasiers arrived at the church, Mimi was being cool but civil toward Adam. Frank, P.W., and Debbie were able to keep a straight face around him. Dress rehearsal was going to require all of their focus and concentration.

Instrumentalists started drifting into the choir room early, leaving behind their cases before heading to the sanctuary. The church deacons had set up snacks in the fellowship hall for later. Since the instrumentalists were professionals, there would be a different break schedule than for a normal St. Cross rehearsal. Union rules had to be followed.

Although this was a smaller crew than the full orchestra Adam had hoped would be playing, the strings, trumpets, a harp, timpani, and organ would be in keeping with the options the 20th-century composer had intended.

Risers for the singers were set up in a wide *U* shape around the front wall of the church. The orchestra members had music stands and folding chairs arrayed on the floor. Adam hunched over his podium, head down, going over his score.

Choir members studied the seating chart and found their places as the first violinist offered the pitch. Adam shushed the singers, and the instrumentalists began tuning up. Mimi took her place at the organ. Adam gave the soloists individual instructions on when to move and where to stand when singing their sections. Pastor Conroy stopped by to cheer on the assembled and offer a brief prayer.

At precisely 7:20 p.m., Adam raised his baton. He counted three silent beats in the air, and the strings began. Four beats later the tenors and basses broke in quietly with their chant-like "requiem aeternam." The women came in a few measures after with a soft angelic "ah" above them. Heads bobbed and bodies swayed in time to the conductor's baton. The choir seemed to breathe and move as one. A few basses had their heads buried in their scores, but for the most part the singers were looking up, watching Adam.

Pastor Conroy stood entranced at the back of

the church, taking in the scene. At night, the ornate sanctuary looked much older than its years, like a cathedral from medieval times. The artificial light cast long shadows. The cross that hung above the choir seemed more prominent, highlighted by its dark shadow against the red velvet backdrop. Temporary lights situated behind the choir shone down on the singer's heads, creating a halo effect.

Adam segued seamlessly into the second movement, the Kyrie. The volume built until the very end, when he ended the piece quietly. After the cutoff, he left his arms raised in the air as a signal for the choir and instrumentalists that they weren't finished until his cue.

The deep silence of the sanctuary sounded almost as beautiful to Pastor Conroy as the music had. Then he heard the wind whistling beyond the boarded-up front door. *Time to hit the road before a storm blows in,* he thought. He quietly turned to exit the sanctuary. As he stepped into the narthex, he did a double-take. Was someone there in the darkness? Had someone else snuck in to listen, as he had? No, he decided, looking around. Just more shadows.

"I am very pleased so far," Adam said, breaking the silence. "Choir, you know what to do. Follow the dynamics as written. Basses, I don't care to look at the tops of your heads. Where are my basses? Raise your hands. Did you adhere to the seating chart? Well, look up or I may throw something at you. A shoe comes to mind. The women don't seem to mind looking at me.

"Strings, we'll take the beginning a little faster next time. It is written as andante moderato. I slowed down a hair for the benefit of the singers and their first time together with you. I'd like to run through the entire Requiem twice tonight if we have time. Let's proceed with the Domine Jesu Christe. Watch my beat.

"Singers, listen to the interplay between the organ and the bass player. Don't just suddenly come to life when it's your turn to sing. Engage! Do you need to watch your score when the instruments are playing? I'll give you your cues. And altos, give me a clear D consonant on Domine at your entrance. I know the volume is piano, but I want a forte consonant."

The choir made it less than halfway into the movement before Adam rapped his baton on the music stand and called the musicians to a halt. "Excuse me, orchestra." He addressed the choir. "Dear singers, do you even remember what you are singing about? You sound so happy. Like children frolicking off for a picnic. You should be terrified. You are beseeching God to spare the faithful dead from the pains of hell, from the deep pit. Here's the translation: Deliver them from the lion's mouth that hell engulf them not, nor shall they fall into darkness."

Just then the lights flickered.

"Nice touch, Edith," Adam said, looking up toward the vaulted ceiling. His comment was met with laughter. "Now, let's take this part again. Eight measures before rehearsal 19 please."

They continued to plow through the music until break time. The conductor excused the orchestra first. "I have just a few spots to review with the choir. And this will give you a head start on grabbing a snack. Once I release the choir, they will descend on the goodies like a plague of locusts. Back in 20 minutes, please."

After the choir was dismissed, Jim caught up with Sammie on the way to the fellowship hall.

"Whaddya think?" he asked. "Pretty cool, huh?"

Sammie seemed a bit distracted. "Oh, yeah. But this place gives me the creeps at night. It looks so ... I don't know ... gothic. Your solo was terrific, by the way. Hey, how'd your finals go?"

They continued their conversation at the snack table. Harper got their attention from farther back in the line.

"Hi Sammie, hi Jim," she said. "Hey listen, Sammie, I forgot to tell you I'm out tomorrow night for a party. Any chance you can move your shift an hour to help take care of closing? No worries, if you already have plans, though."

Sammie looked at Jim. "Nope. None so far. Sure thing, Harper."

"Thanks, Sammie."

Before long, break was over and the second half of rehearsal was underway. Adam decided to pick up from the third movement at the moderato to let the sopranos have another stab at their entrance. Mimi deftly played the notes that led them in. Jim picked up his solo after the soprano line. His deep bass voice resounded throughout the sanctuary. After working through the rest of the Requiem with a minimum of interruptions and repeats, Adam placed his baton on the music stand.

"I must say this has come together much better than I anticipated," he said. "I expect you all to be on your game for the concert. Call time is 5 p.m. for the 8 p.m. performance. We'll break for dinner from 7 to 7:45 so you can change and have a bite to eat. Pack a sack supper. I don't want anyone fainting during the show."

The wind had picked up throughout the evening, and rain was starting to fall. As the conductor moved to dismiss the orchestra a flash of lightning illuminated the church interior. Seconds later a clap of thunder shook the building.

Harper involuntarily jumped and made a sound. She'd had enough of lightning and thunder recently. Frank looked over in her direction from his spot among the men, but couldn't make eye contact. She looked as if she had seen a ghost.

"Apparently Edith approves," Adam said. "I do believe that's her idea of applause. Be gone now."

The words were barely out of his mouth when the lights flickered and went out entirely. A collective groan rose from the chorus. After a long anxious moment, the emergency lighting came on.

"Shall we make that, be gone now, quickly?" Adam said. Few wasted time exiting the sanctuary.

Frank, however, needed to reset the fuse box. He also wanted to check on Harper. He just wasn't sure in what order to accomplish those tasks.

The two hadn't really discussed their ill-fated adventure in the storm on the mountain. He had been a real grouch as his foot healed. Plus the painkillers weren't really agreeing with him, so he'd kept to himself. But Frank was familiar with post-traumatic stress syndrome from his own life experience, and it occurred to him that the thunder and lightning might be especially unnerving to her.

"Harper," he yelled, seeing her pale face as she headed for the door. "You got a minute?"

She looked torn but turned back to face him. "Howdy, stranger," she said. Worried she sounded irritated, she followed with a more casual: "What can I do you for?"

"I just wanted to see how you're doing, but I need to reset the fuse box," he said. The rehearsal had lasted past 10 p.m., and Harper was exhausted. *Why now,* she thought. *You've had all week to see how I'm doing.*

"As you like," she said.

The pair picked their way through the half-lit hallway that led to the fellowship hall, then to the far corner of the room to a plain-looking door.

"Utility room," Frank said. "Let me get these lights restored, then I'll close up and walk you to your car."

A new round of thunder startled Harper. Suddenly she was tired of it all. Tired of Frank's lack of communication and what seemed to her a somewhat controlling nature. Tired of herself for trotting after him like a star-struck school girl when he beckoned. Tired of being in unfamiliar and sometimes dangerous situations.

Frank flipped the fuse-box switch.

"I'm tired," Harper said, tersely. "You said you wanted to see how I'm doing. Well, I'm tired."

A sharp crack of thunder rattled the windows in the building. "And if I hear any more thunder, I'm going to crawl out of my skin." Harper was shaking.

Frank grasped both her forearms. "I was worried about this," he said. "Out. We're out of here as quick as I can close up." He took her hand, and they literally ran from one door to another as fast as his injured foot would allow, doubling-checking that all the exits were locked. Then they dashed for her car, the rain pelting down on them. Frank shoved Harper into the passenger seat and grabbed her car keys from her hand. She was gulping for air and couldn't form the words to protest.

"What's happening?" she managed to ask.

"Harper, look at me," Frank said, holding her shoulders. "I think you may be having a panic attack. Do you have any bags in the car?"

She motioned to the driver side door. "Doggie," she said.

"That'll do," Frank said. "Now I want you to breathe into the bag. In and out, slowly, in and out. You're moving too much oxygen, and you're hyperventilating. Have you ever had an anxiety attack before?"

Harper shook her head no.

"Well, I have," Frank said. "They are no fun, believe me, but you'll get through this. And you don't have to do this alone. I'm here. We'll get you through this together."

Even with the windshield wipers at high speed, Frank could see just a few feet ahead of the vehicle. Harper removed the bag. "Your truck," she said.

Frank hushed her and stopped to place the

bag back over her mouth. "Try to slow down your breathing," he said. "This should pass in a few minutes. I'll take you home, and if we need to we'll call in the professionals."

By the time they wound up Harper's driveway, her breathing was returning to normal. Despite the heat being on full blast, however, she was shaking. "How did you know?" she asked through chattering teeth.

"I didn't," Frank said as he hustled her inside. "But I saw the way you jumped at the first clap of thunder, and it occurred to me the storm might trigger a panic attack. Something similar happened to me before."

Once inside he sat her on the couch and wrapped her in a quilt. Then he ducked into the back of the house, found the master bathroom and starting drawing a hot bath. After lighting the wood she had already stacked in the fireplace, he ushered her into the back and pulled off her shoes, socks and sweater.

"Now you do the rest and yell out to me when you are in the tub," he said, dipping a finger into the water to make sure he hadn't gotten it too hot. She was in no shape to argue.

He stood, ear to the door until she yelled. "I'm in."

"Good," he said. "I'm going to scour the kitchen for a hot drink or some soup. I won't be gone long."

Herbal tea was the best he could do. A few minutes later he was back outside her bathroom door. He could hear Harper sobbing inside. *Maybe this isn't the best plan,* he thought.

"Harper, I've got hot tea ready for you in the living room and the fire is roaring," Frank yelled from her bedroom. "If you're warmed up, pull a towel over yourself or something."

There was no answer.

"Are you okay? I'm coming in."

"No, don't," she said, sobbing. "This is just too embarrassing." He paused.

"You still have the shakes?" he asked.

"A bit," she said. "Frank, this doesn't make sense. What is going on with me?"

"It's different for everybody. See if you can stand. Take it slowly."

Harper found she could navigate her way out of the water. She toweled off and studied her rain-soaked clothes on the floor.

"I need some dry things," she said, trying to keep her breathing steady.

Frank pulled open some drawers and selected sweat pants, warm socks and a baggy sweater. He thought it would be too invasive to go pawing through her underwear drawer. He cracked the door and passed them through. "Holler when you're ready, and I'll walk you to the living room. No fainting will be allowed unless I'm there to catch you."

She dressed as quickly as she could under the circumstances, but found she was already getting cold again. "Holler," she said weakly.

He opened the door and gently steered her to a spot in front of the fire where he had laid a quilt. The hot tea was on the hearth. He positioned her in front of the fire and sat down behind her, straddling her with his legs and wrapping his arms around her once-again shaking body. Sometimes he rubbed her shoulders, his breath warm on her neck. But mostly they sat, rocking gently.

"Try to drink this," he said, handing her the tea.

Harper gradually stopped shaking, and her breath, ragged from crying, eventually returned to normal. She felt anything but okay, however. A fatigue unlike any she had ever experienced seemed to have invaded every molecule of her body. She was nodding off as Frank lifted her up and placed her on the couch. He tucked several blankets around her and stroked her hair for a long time.

Then he turned the heat up in the house and went to straighten the bathroom.

The storm was over. He left his phone number in big bold letters by her landline and turned on the goose-neck desk light. Then he slipped her house key off the chain and left the others on the note.

Frank stepped outside and locked the front

door. He pulled out his phone and punched in a familiar number. A sheriff's department dispatcher answered. "Hey, Lydia," he said in a quiet voice. "This is Frank O'Brien. I'm over at Harper Henshaw's place on Sierra Drive. Yeah, the new gal's house. I took her home after rehearsal when she fell ill, but now I'm kind of stranded over here. My ride is at the church.

"I'm gonna try to hoof it back there. Can you let your patrol officer know I would appreciate a lift if and when he's not otherwise engaged?

"Yeah. Okay. Thanks."

Frank headed off in the direction of the church, mentally calculating how long it would take to walk there. His exhalations were visible in the cold night air. Stars were starting to peek through the firmament as the clouds cleared. After about 10 minutes, a black-and-white pulled up behind him, lights flashing.

"Nice touch," Frank said, hopping into the passenger seat. He recognized the rookie cop. Russell Wilson was in his late 20s. The officer killed the flashers, and they drove in silence to the church. The police radio crackled off and on. Frank was glad for the heat and the lift. His foot ached. He was looking forward to getting home and taking a painkiller. Why hadn't he brought them with him?

As Russell swung into the church parking lot something caught his eye in the direction of the graveyard. Frank saw it, too. The officer turned off the car and pulled the radio to his mouth. "At the church. Going to take a walk around to make sure the premises are secure."

"10-4," came the reply.

He turned to Frank. "What did you make of that?" he asked. "That green glow."

Frank stroked his chin. "Seems way too early in the year for foxfire."

"What's that?" the rookie asked.

"A type of fungus in decaying wood that can give off a glow," Frank said. "But you never know with the electrical storm and all. There's a motion-sensitive light at the back of the church building. Maybe it's reflecting the ground fog."

The pair stepped out of the cruiser. "Think I'll just check things out," Russell said.

Frank felt for the rookie. St. Cross Church could be an eerie place at night, especially if one bought into the stories of sightings of Edith. No doubt senior officers had filled the young man's head with their tall tales. Frank figured he owed Russell a favor.

"Tell you what," he said. "I've got church keys, so what say I join you in case you need to gain access for any reason."

The cop nodded affirmatively and raised his hand to quiet Frank. Apparently this was going to be a stealth operation. Frank grinned in the dark in spite of himself. *Poor guy,* he thought.

As they approached the graveyard the glow seemed to diminish. Russell shone his high-beam flashlight over the stone slabs. Suddenly movement caught their eyes. Perched at the base of Edith Saint Cross' tombstone was a raven or small crow. Frank couldn't tell which. Perhaps startled by the light, the bird took flight and flapped away into the night.

"Of all things," Frank said, as he headed for his truck.

21

Frank called on Harper about 11 the next morning, with biscuits-and-gravy in a plastic takeout container and two coffees.

She opened the door on the first knock.

"Hey, there," he said. "Feeling any better today?" He handed her the house key.

"Oh, Frank," she said. "Thanks so much for stopping in, and for last night. I don't know what to say."

He looked at her with concern. "You just said it. Now do you think you can get some food down?"

"Yes," she said, opening the door wider to let him pass. "I'm ravenous."

Harper had obviously been up for a while. Her wet hair indicated that she had showered. She was wearing jeans and a sweatshirt. The living room curtains were open, letting in the late-morning sunshine. The light played on the strands of her red hair, making some of the drying tips appear golden as Frank followed her to the small dining room table.

They settled in and made small talk as she ate. Mostly they sat in silence, enjoying the quiet that filled the bungalow. Frank studied the oil paintings she had hung on the walls. He wondered if she was a painter. For all they had been through in their brief time together, he felt he knew very little about her. In fact, he wasn't sure what she had even ordered for breakfast when they'd eaten out a few weeks earlier. Without thinking, he had ordered the biscuits and gravy – a favorite comfort food of his wife, Teresa.

"Harper," Frank said as she stopped between bites. He gently placed his fingertips on top of her hand. "You're gonna need some help with this. Do you have a doctor in town yet?"

She drew her hand back and rubbed the top of it for fear she would cry. His unexpected kindness touched her deeply. "No, but I can contact my old psychologist and get a referral. I've been in treatment for depression, with my folks dying and all."

"Good," Frank replied, standing to rise. He looked solid and outdoorsy in his plaid shirt and khaki pants. "I'm sorry, but I've gotta scoot.

Apparently I said I was giving a party tonight. What *was* I thinking?

"I hope you'll still come if you're feeling up to it. Don't worry about bringing anything or arriving early to help me get ready. Just take of yourself today.

"Oh, and Harper? If I were you, I'd check one or two of the 'guests' out of that hotel you run. Temporary foster. Dogs helped me a lot when I was healing. I used to rotate them in and out until I settled on Grin and Barrett."

Harper nodded and watched him walk out the door. A smile played at the corners of her mouth. *That paper-towel guy,* she thought. *Frank looks a bit like that lumberjack in those ads*. She tried to remember the pitchline. *He has the strength to conquer any ... kitchen mess.* She'd keep that mind.

Oh, I am seriously losing it, she thought, but laughed anyway. The sound reverberated through her small house.

The day was a blur for Frank. He laid in ice, set up two charcoal grills and made sure the bun to bratwurst numbers added up. Some guests were bringing appetizers and dessert, so he focused on making two large bowls of coleslaw and found room for them in the fridge. Then he put beer and ale in several coolers to chill, along with bottles of water. *Flatware, plates, napkins,* he ran down the list. *Check, check, check.* The last thing he did was set up the coffee urn he had borrowed from the church. He'd return the old machine cleaner than he found it. There was time left to shower. He'd put the chips out, open the mustards, and light some candles right before the first guests arrived.

Harper spent a good part of her day sitting in the sun on her front porch, wrapped in a quilt. She had no energy and quickly lost interest in anything she tried to do. Even reading seemed too taxing. Listening to the birdsong and the chatter of chipmunks felt incredibly calming, so she immersed herself into just being in her surroundings.

Finally she pulled out her smart phone and made a call for a late-afternoon manicure, pedicure, and hair styling. The day seemed as good a time as any to treat herself.

When Harper arrived at Frank's house, the party was well underway. He was playing the good host, circulating among his guests and making sure they knew where the drinks and food were. Grin and Barrett were wearing themselves out by sniffing new arrivals and proffering kisses to anyone who bent down to lick level.

"Harper!" he said, greeting her with a hug. "You look great. I'm so glad you came. It's kind of noisy and crowded up here, but there are probably still places to sit in the downstairs family room if you don't feel like standing. I'm kind of stuck at the door greeting. Hans, can you show Harper the way? And get her something to drink?"

"Glad to help out, Frankie," Hans said jovially, clapping Frank on the back. "I finally have a chance to get acquainted with the mysterious new woman in town. Welcome. I am Hans. We met briefly when you brought Frank back from the hospital."

Harper looked up at the man, who seemed like a different person cleaned up and out of his work clothes. Hans also seemed to be nearly two feet taller than she was. He looked somewhat Nordic or Germanic. His accented English gave her a starting point.

"You don't sound like you originated here," Harper said over the din as she trailed him to the bar area. She grabbed a bottle of water. Hans selected a craft beer.

"No, I did not," he said. "Swedish is my first language, but I'm also fluent in German and obviously English. Although you might question my English if we talk for a very long time."

They made their way downstairs. Hans motioned to one remaining spot on the couch. "You take it," Harper said, "and I'll sit on the arm. Otherwise I'm going to end up with a terrific neck-ache from looking up at you."

Their conversation was easy and casual. Hans was a fire-prevention officer with the Forest Service. His time was split between actually suppressing fires and educating the public. He particularly enjoyed going into classrooms and working with the different grade-levels.

"Harper, you are new here," he said. "I'd be happy to come by your house and see what might be done on your property to minimize fire danger. That's another big part of my job, as well as enforcement.

"I could write you a ticket," he said, laughing at his own joke.

"Gee, thanks," Harper said. "But it would be good to have a trained eye take a look around. I've been so focused on the interiors and needed repairs. Let me know when it's convenient."

"Well, I always say no time like the present," he said, "but it's dark now and I am at a party. How about next Friday? I'll come by in the late afternoon and give you my assessment. In the meantime, would you like to go out for dinner Sunday night?"

Between his slight accent and the increasing noise level, Harper wasn't quite sure she heard him correctly.

"Pardon me?" she asked, not wanting to

make a fool of herself by taking him up on an offer that hadn't been made.

"Dinner," he said. "This Sunday. I can come by about 5:30, and we'll go grab an early supper. Have you been to the Stock Exchange? 'The oldest continually operating restaurant in town,' or so the marquee reads. Apparently the establishment was very popular with early ranchers."

"Sure," Harper said. "Why not?"

"Now let me introduce you around," he said. "I shouldn't keep you all to myself."

Harper's head was spinning. *What a place,* she thought. *In 24 hours I've had my worst experience since I moved here, and been asked on my first date in years.*

Hans and Harper eventually made their way back upstairs. Apparently Frank had given her full credit for her part in rescuing Sheldon and helping him back to safety. Hans kept introducing her as the woman who saved Frank to roars of laughter, to wisecracks, or to raised eyebrows. A few of the guests told Harper that Frank was beyond salvage.

Finally Hans excused himself, and Harper had a minute alone. She spotted Jessica coming in the front door. Frank greeted the off-duty sheriff's deputy with a long embrace. Another woman coming in right after her got a side hug and a peck on the cheek. *Someone should do a sociological study on what it all means,* Harper thought.

"Jessie," she called out, waving the blonde over. "You look fantastic! Love those boots."

"Thanks," Jessica said. "Sorry to be arriving late. Frank always gives a great party but just not very often, so I hate to miss a minute. But I got held up at work. Hey, meet my partner, Loretta. I'll just go grab us some beers."

Jessie scooted off to the bar, and Harper greeted the fit brunette. "That's pretty neat," Harper said. "With so few women on the force, how nice you could partner with another woman."

Loretta looked at her in silence, then started laughing. "No, no. Not that kind of partner," she said. "I'm not on the force. I'm Jessie's 'significant other.' "

Harper felt herself blush at the faux pas. "Oh, I'm such an idiot," Harper said, remembering that at the dinner party she assumed Loretta was Jessica's pet dog. "I misunderstood."

"I'm a contractor actually," Loretta said. "I'm kind of surprised Frank didn't tell you about Jessie and me. Jessie said she thought you and Frank were getting pretty close."

"Ah, well," Harper said, "ever the gentleman. We have been through some interesting experiences together, but I'd say it's too soon to know if we'll be close.

"And no," Harper said, "he didn't mention you and Jessie were together. Just that the two of them broke up a few years back and the reason why was hers to tell."

"How chivalrous," Loretta said. "Well, now you know. Sounds like you and Frank have at least advanced to the 'past loves' confession stage. You two have been kind of the subject of some of the town gossips – they think he's going for you."

"What?" Harper said. "He's spent about 30 seconds with me all night. Foisted me off on Hans."

"Well, you could do worse," Loretta said. "Frank's a whole lotta man to handle. You know, complicated, issues, ego. I'm starved. Let's grab something to eat."

Over brats and beer they discussed the bids on Harper's home improvement projects, then Loretta filled her in on other local hearsay. "You're in the choir, right," Loretta said, although she knew the answer. "Well, I hear you have to watch yourself around Adam – has a roving eye and hands to match."

"Really?" Harper said, incredulously. "He seems quite the professional conductor and very devoted to his art."

"I don't make up these rumors," Loretta said. "I just spread them around."

As the time neared 11, the crowd thinned. Hans said his goodbyes to Harper and left with her phone number. Frank shut down the grills, and a few guys took bags of trash out to his bear-proof dumpster. Harper was tidying up in the kitchen when Frank found her.

"Hey, Harper, you don't have to do that," he said, coming up from behind and cupping one of her elbows with his hand. "You're probably tired."

"I don't mind," Harper said. "I had a great time meeting so many interesting people tonight. The prospect of going home to my cold, empty house seemed so .... " She let the sentence hang, unsure of the word she sought and mentally berating herself for starting down this road. She sounded so desperate.

"That's why you need a dog or two from the shelter," he said. "Or at least a cat." Frank looked at her encouragingly. "You'll never come home to an empty house again."

"I'll think about it," she said, folding the dish towel she held and leaving it on the counter. "Thanks again, Frank. I better be off. We have our performance tomorrow night."

He followed her to the front door and touched her upper arm just as she was stepping out. He waited to speak until he was looking directly into her eyes. *What is it with this guy and eye contact,* Harper thought. "Anytime you need a friend, I'm only a call away," he said. "Night or day."

She broke away from his piercing gaze, said "Thanks," and headed into the pitch-black night.

22

Harper was feeling more like her old self the next morning. The dawn brought sunshine and a cloudless sky. The weather forecast showed late-afternoon clouds but no rain or thunderstorms.

Since it was the day of the Duruflé concert she took it easy, setting out her black formal wear and going over her music. The choir call time was 5 p.m. with a break for dinner, so she packed a snack.

She hadn't performed in a major choral work for at least a decade and found the prospect exhilarating. She loved the payback for all the hard work when a performance came together. *Tonight will be terrific,* she thought, as she put on her makeup.

At the Frasier household, the at-odds spouses assumed the roles of professional musicians with a job to do. They reviewed their scores together.

"Watch me here because the instrumentalists tend to lag," Adam said, pointing to a spot in the Sanctus. "They anticipate the ritardando before I've actually given it. Then they slow down too much. We may have to adjust."

In their musical lives, Mimi and Adam were well suited, a solid team. Her depth of talent was a match for his, and one of the reasons Adam had fallen for the serious organist.

For her part, Mimi wondered what had happened to the Adam she first knew. He had been so attentive, pursuing her relentlessly until she accepted his marriage proposal. But there had been so many betrayals since she caught the eye of the confident, dynamic conductor. That he had strayed pointed to a problem in their marriage or within one of them. She didn't know which.

Yet his infidelity hadn't changed her views on his musical genius or their continued union. She believed wedding vows were for life, and eventually, if she was good enough, loyal, and patient, Adam would see the folly in his philandering and recommit to her. Tonight, at least, would unite them through their mutual love of great music, she thought, even if the moment was fleeting.

In his college dorm room, Jim was having a beer and admiring himself in the tuxedo he had borrowed from an upperclassman in the school chamber group. He'd have to get his own tux if he was going to keep singing.

Jim mentally ran through his notes as he fumbled with his bow tie.

His dorm room door burst open, and one of his hall-mates tossed a football in to him, almost knocking over his beer.

"Cut that out," Jim said. "I'm getting dressed here."

He studied his reflection in the mirror and attempted to smooth out some errant hairs on the side of his head. *I'm killin' it tonight,* he thought, looking forward to his first college solo.

And so it went, around town, as chorus members, instrumentalists, ushers, and others prepared for the concert. Different ages, races, and religions were drawing together to create something larger than themselves. Each had a part to do – a role that, whether small or large, was vital to the whole.

Frank arrived early to open up and make sure the physical plant was in order. Harper stopped at the pound to see that staff was in place, then headed for the church for the rehearsal.

The run-through went smoothly, and Adam was pleased. Several faculty members would be in attendance, and the combined college and community effort would further bolster his stock with the dean. He was not above a little one-upmanship within his department. He played to win.

The dreaded Cecelia had thus far not followed through with her blackmail threat. The women he bedded rarely caused much trouble. Tears, screaming, and pounding fists seemed to be the worst of it. His present and future were secure.

Before Adam excused the chorus for dinner, he offered a few words.

"I want you to take a look at the person to your right. Now, your left. Look at the one in front of you and the one behind. This is the last time you will rehearse with this choir. Never again will this particular group be assembled in this manner. Today we will have the privilege of an audience, and the performance will be the last time you sing with these voices. After tonight this unique sound to which you all contribute will be extinguished for all time. Make the music matter, dear singers. You owe that much to yourselves, each other, the audience, and the glory of God."

The choir erupted into applause before recessing to change and have a bite to eat.

When Frank wandered outside during the break, he realized law enforcement was on the premises with a K9 unit. He didn't recognize the officers with the beagles, but he knew the cop who had given him the ride two nights earlier. Russ stood outside his cruiser, watching the action. Frank sauntered over.

"What do they expect to find?" he asked. "There have been a zillion people through here since the vandalism."

"These aren't trackers," Russ said. "They're detection or sniffer dogs looking for drugs. Following up on a phone tip that came in."

"They're looking for drugs outside the church?" Frank asked.

Russ shrugged. "That was the tip: supposed drop point," he said. "Caller was sloppy, and we got a trace. Maybe we'll get lucky. Dogs were in town anyway for another operation, so we thought it was worth a shot."

"So, no relation to the vandalism incident?" Frank asked, not sure what to make of it all.

Russ shrugged and walked off toward the other officers.

The cops were gone by the time 7:30 rolled around. People started arriving early for the performance.

Aza was dressed up in a navy blue suit since he would be "helping" the older boys usher. Actually P.W. was paying one of the teenagers to keep an eye on the lad. The back of Aza's too-long pants dragged on the floor.

The instrumentalists, outfitted in black formal wear, took their spots. At 8 sharp the choir filed in. The lights dimmed.

Pastor Conroy approached the front in his black robe. He said a few words and offered a prayer before the performance. Light shone on the front of the sanctuary, leaving the back bathed in shadows.

Adam entered and walked stalwartly to the podium. He raised his baton, and with a movement from his arms the beauty of the music began to wash over the audience. Sound and time played against each other until they became intertwined. He let the score guide him, marveling at the ethereal moments that followed one after another like links in a chain. In what to him seemed like both no time at all and an eternity, the last note was fading, the performance over.

Adam kept his arms stretched out long after the last note diminished. He often found the silence after organized sound to be spiritually uplifting. *Glorious*, he thought, and lowered his baton. He dropped his head, spent from the experience.

The audience exploded into enthusiastic applause. By all accounts, the evening had been a success. And yet, Adam was unsettled. He looked over at Mimi seated at the organ console. He nodded to his wife, and she returned the gesture with a slight bow on the head. Then he turned to face the audience and motioned for her to rise to be acknowledged. Adam did the same with the soloists, then the orchestra, and finally the entire choir.

When the applause died down he strode toward Mimi. He knew what he had to do. The time had come to make amends.

As the choir exited in a line, Sammie broke ranks to greet her parents. She was actually a little sad that this phase of her "punishment" was over.

"Let me just say goodbye to some of the choir members and then I'll be ready to go," she said to her mother. "I'll look for you at the reception in fellowship hall."

In the choir room she found Jim turning in his music.

"Hey, Jim," she said tentatively. "Great job tonight."

"Thanks, Sammie," he said. "Actually I can't believe it's over, and I won't be seeing you on Thursday nights anymore. Three more months of school, and I'll be back home for a summer job – unless I can find one here."

"I know," she said in a dispirited voice. Actually, she didn't know and hadn't thought that far ahead. "I hope you'll come by and see me. Grab a root beer maybe?"

"You bet," he said and stole a quick kiss.

Harper watched the interaction from across the room, feeling a bit like a voyeur. She was glad Sammie had made a friend. Right then, she and Sammie didn't seem so very different from each other, even though they were decades apart in age. Both were trying to figure out life, fit in, and understand men.

As Harper put her coat on, the domineering Judy Carey stopped her to ask if she was going to the reception.

"Oh, well, I didn't really have anyone in the audience," Harper said.

"You most certainly did," Judy said. "You had the whole town out there. Now, come on. You are a part of us now."

Harper meekly followed Judy to the

fellowship hall. The words played in a loop in her head. "You are a part of us now." *Part of a bunch of imperfect folks trying to pick their way through each day as best they can,* she thought.

The Requiem had worked its magic. Harper felt a part of something larger than herself here in this church choir and in this town. She felt like she belonged.

After the reception, an exhausted P.W. buckled a sugar-fueled Aza into their truck. He listened quietly as he drove while the boy rambled on about the evening. Try as he might, P.W. couldn't seem to stay focused on what the boy was saying. He hadn't told Frank why he asked him to watch Aza that Saturday, and at first thought he'd keep it that way. But the vandalism at the church and Adam's attempt at an overthrow were weighing on his mind.

P.W. had gone into Alta that day for a complete physical and on legal business. He was concerned about his memory, which wasn't nearly as sharp as it used to be. All the test results came back within normal limits, and the doctor felt his minor memory loss was in keeping with his years. The doc had said the fact that P.W. was concerned about his memory was a good sign. If he had Alzheimer's, for example, he'd most likely be defensive and adamantly dispute that there was anything wrong with his brain.

Somehow P.W. found no solace in the information. He knew his mind was slipping.

He wondered if he had it in him to raise a teenager. Before long Aza could be giving him real trouble. P.W. wasn't the same man he was a decade earlier, when he took the boy in. P.W. had slowed down considerably.

By the time he got Aza inside and to bed, every muscle in P.W.'s back hurt. Although he was in pain, P.W. dozed off soon after he rested his head on the pillow.

23

Sleep came slowly to Harper. *Singing for several hours must super-oxygenate one's blood,* she thought. She could never rest well after rehearsals, so why would the night of a performance be any different? Waking up in time for Sunday church services seemed a very remote possibility.

Eventually Harper fell into a fitful sleep and then drifted deeper. In her dream Edith Saint Cross was looking down on her as she slept while a phone rang nearby. The ghostly presence shook her head from side to side as if to say "Don't answer that" before she faded away.

Harper realized she was awake and in fact her phone was ringing. *What time is it,* she wondered as her eyes focused on the illuminated bedside clock. "Three a.m.?" she said and answered the phone. "Hello?"

"Silver Glen Security Services," said a male voice on the other end. "Is this Harper Henshaw?"

"Yes," she said. "Why are you calling here?"

"Security breach at the animal shelter, ma'am," the caller said. "Usually I'd call Frank O'Brien, but the computer brought up your name."

"Yes, I'm the new manager," Harper said. "What's the procedure? Does this happen a lot?"

"Usually we can have a car to the shelter within 10 to 20 minutes, but the only vehicle we have near your area is just leaving an incident on the other side of the mountain. Our ETA is 45 minutes.

"We'll alert the sheriff's department of our delay, so they'll no doubt beat us to the scene. As for how often this happens, let me take a quick look in the database."

Harper switched on her bedside lamp and waited while the dispatcher clicked computer keys.

"You've had almost no false alarms out there. In the last three years, calls were due to a transient entering the premises, wildlife trying to get at the shelter animals and, once, a power surge set off the bells and whistles."

"I'm sorry I'm so ignorant about all this,"

Harper said. "Will an alarm be sounding and disturbing the animals or is this a silent system?"

"Let me check," he said. "Look like it's an intermittent beep, ma'am, with a manual shut off right on the box."

"Well, I suppose I should head out there then and turn it off," Harper said. "I know where the box is."

"Ma'am," he said, "we don't recommend getting there ahead of our car or law enforcement, for your personal safety. If you do decide to go over, give it a 10-minute rest before you head out."

"Thank you," Harper said. "I'll do that. You've been very helpful."

"Oh, and ma'am: Is this a landline or a cell?"

"It's my cell."

"Perfect. I'll call this number if there are any developments."

Harper wiggled into some jeans and a sweatshirt. She took her time pulling on socks and lacing her work boots.

This seems to be one part of the job Frank forgot to tell me about, she thought as she splashed water on her face and ran a comb through her hair. "That cuts it," she said to her reflection. "No church for me this morning." She remembered a saying her mother used on the rare Sunday they would miss services when she was growing up. "It'll be Bedside Baptist today, Pastor Sheets presiding."

Even delaying her departure and accounting for the car ride, Harper beat the sheriff to the shelter parking lot. Her first thought was to wait in her car, doors locked. But then movement caught her eye, and she didn't like what she was seeing: dogs. Dogs in the yard, dogs outside their runs, dogs everywhere except where they were supposed to be.

"Damn it," she said, jumping out of her car. Mrs. Zelinsky's ancient corgi ambled past her. She grabbed the dog's collar and tugged it toward the front door. To her surprise, the door was locked. She fumbled with her keys at first, then once inside she switched on the lights. Shutting the door behind her, she pulled her cell out of her pocket and found Frank's number. He grumbled a reply on the second ring.

"Dogs. Out. Everywhere. At the shelter," she said.

"What are you doing there this time of night?" Frank asked, shaking his head to clear his thoughts. "Dumb question. On my way." He hung up.

Harper surveyed the situation. The corgi would be safe in the office reception area. She'd just shut the dog in for the moment. Moving behind the counter, she opened the door to the hall that went past the cat house and animal bathing area, flipping on lights as she went. Several of the cats seemed agitated but they at least were in their enclosures.

The shrill beep of the alarm sounded, and Harper jumped.

When she entered the hall lined with dog kennels, the scene became chaotic. The locks had been destroyed on nearly every kennel, and the doors stood open. A few animals remained in their pens, so she closed those up first. She'd worry about locks later. The exit at the end of the hall stood open. *That's probably what tripped the alarm,* she thought. She pulled the door shut and entered the storage room to disable the signal. The sound was getting to her. Then she only had to contend with the incessant barking.

Harper was more concerned about the dogs outside than those wandering the kennel hall. She grabbed a half-dozen leashes and bolted out the back. She hoped no fights would break out among the uncaged animals left inside.

The moonless night made it hard for her eyes to adjust after being in the well-lit kennel. A thin husky she at first mistook for a wolf stared her down. The canine offered little resistance to being leashed, however, and shoved into the kennel hall with the others.

Then she second-guessed her approach. *This is nuts,* Harper thought, *I should kennel them as I go. And I need more help.*

She turned to reenter the kennel when a man stepped out from behind the open back door. He was restraining two dogs by their collars, a terrier mix with one hand and, with the other, the kennel's lone Presa Canario: the evidence dogs.

"Leash 'em," he said in a low growl.

Stunned, Harper complied. "Um, you actually can't handle those dogs, only I can. They're being held in connection with an ongoing investigation." Even as she said the words she realized how inane they sounded.

"I can handle 'em," he said in a mocking voice. "My dogs."

A shiver ran through her as a tiny Jack Russell terrier rushed to her side and started barking at the larger dogs.

"Shut the rat up before I do," the stranger said. He had moved both of the leashed dogs to his left hand and was holding something she couldn't quite make out in his right.

She snatched up the Jack Russell, holding it close to her chest and quieting the dog. She doubted the small terrier would be much of a shield for a bullet shot at close range.

The intruder motioned for her to go inside through the back door. Harper stepped toward it just as a truck pulled into the parking lot. The stranger took a stride away to get a better look at the vehicle. Harper launched the Jack Russell in his direction and used the diversion to bolt for the door. Once inside, she flipped the deadbolt. Her heart was pounding.

The front is locked, the back is locked, she mentally checked off. Next she started checking the locks on all the windows while trying to stay out of sight.

Above the barking dogs she heard what sounded like someone trying to pound down the front door.

"Harper, Harper," Frank shouted. "Are you okay?"

"Yes," she screamed, running to the reception area. She flipped the dead bolt, and her legs turned to jelly. Frank barely caught her as she fell to the floor. "Lock it, lock it. He's out there," she managed to say.

Frank locked them back in and joined her on the floor. "I think he left when I pulled in. There was a truck out back that pulled away. Who would do this?"

"Evidence dogs," she said, panting. "He took the evidence dogs."

"Whoa," Frank said. "Slow down. Where's the security company? Where are the cops?"

"I don't know," Harper said. "Dogs are everywhere."

"Okay," Frank said, moving into methodical mode. "Let's get the ones that are inside back into their kennels, starting with this corgi. We can't do anything for the dogs outside until sheriff's deputies arrive and secure the area. Let me call 911 first."

Harper tried to catch her breath while Frank shouted into the phone.

"What do you mean they're all out?" he said. "Then get the desk sergeant over here if you have to, for Christ's sake."

Once off the line, he steadied his voice and turned to Harper. "I feel like I've just been put on hold by 911. Apparently the big drug cartel bust went down tonight. We're on our own for another 10 to 15 minutes."

Frank pulled Harper up by her hand and assessed her. "You want to take a seat while I sort out this chaos?" he asked.

"No, I'm okay," she said. "I'd like to keep busy."

Together they scooped up dog after dog and placed each in a kennel. They'd sort out which dog ended up in which enclosure later.

Frank broke up one scuffle between two female shepherd mixes before it escalated. A few males appeared to have already battled and worked out their differences. One had a bright red gash on his ear. Blood dripped on the concrete floor.

"Harper, call the vet over in Riverdale," Frank said. "See if they can send someone over. There may be other injuries. Then see what you can do with that laceration. Ear wounds bleed a lot."

They were kenneling the last of the indoor dogs as Frank heard the approach of sirens. "About time."

24

Harper was at the shelter until 6 a.m., rounding up dogs and giving a report to law enforcement. Buck showed up for the early shift and surveyed the hasty rearrangement of the dogs.

"Holy shit," he said when Harper briefed him about the night's events. "This is going to take some sorting out. How many dogs are we still missing?"

"Three, besides the two that were taken," she said in an exhausted haze. "Frank left more than an hour ago in search of them, but hasn't come back."

Buck's new energy filled the void created by her lack of momentum.

"I'll email all staff and volunteers to be on the lookout," he said. "And I'll put out the word that we can use extra help today. I'd like every one of these dogs to have a good looking-over so we don't miss any injuries. We'll need to re-tag all the kennels and re-enter the info into the computer. In the meantime, I'll tie off all these doors with twine so the dogs can't rattle them open.

"You, on the other hand, look beat. Why don't you go home and catch a few?" he said. "I'll text if there are any developments, so you can rest. I won't call unless there's an emergency."

Harper nodded gratefully. "Thank you, Buck," she said. "You're a lifesaver."

"Get outta here," he said. "I've got this under control."

It was mid-afternoon by the time Harper awoke. She scanned her texts. Nothing urgent required her attention. Sheriff's deputies had been at the pound most of the day, taking photos of the truck's tire tracks and dusting for fingerprints. Harper and Frank had taken something of a tongue lashing in the early morning hours for "contaminating" the crime scene, but the welfare of the dogs had been their priority, not police work. In her fatigue she had forgotten to warn Buck about that. *Oh well,* she thought, *he can handle himself.*

Two of the three errant dogs had been found and returned to the shelter, Buck had texted. Only one remained missing, if you didn't count the evidence dogs. Unfortunately, it was the pregnant beagle.

Harper had thrown off her soiled clothes when she collapsed into bed. As the room had warmed up throughout the day, they had started to let off dog and kennel odors. She fought back against her gag reflex. After shoving them into the washing machine, Harper drew a bath for herself. A groggy and grimy face stared back at her from the mirror. Grabbing a washcloth, she eased herself into the hot water for a well-deserved soak.

Scrubbed and ready to face what was left of the day, Harper couldn't quite figure out what to do with her time. Her brain was racing, from one train of thought to the next. She paced a bit and then put her restless energy to use straightening up the house and moving the laundry along.

Before the kennel closed, she made a call.

"Vi," Harper said. Of course the dependable staffer had come in to help sort out the mess. "Did Mrs. Zelinsky's corgi get adopted today?"

"Not one adoption, but lots of people came through," Vi said, "to gossip and see for themselves. Not sure what they expected. Place is pretty well back in order."

"I'm taking the corgi. Please put a hold on her," Harper said. "What name does she go by?"

"Delilah," came the answer. "Shall I mark her for temporary foster?"

"No," Harper said. "I'm adopting her. She'll be mine. I'll take her home tomorrow."

"That's swell, Mrs. Henshaw, I mean Harper," Vi said. "I'll give you a call if one comes in named Samson."

Harper laughed, then she rang off. She held her head in her hands, trying to figure out the next step. *Me,* she thought, *I'm the next step.* Harper turned to her contact list and found the name of her old psychologist. She placed a call and left a message.

After one more tear through the house, putting away anything she could find that was out of place, Harper plopped on the couch and turned on the television. When the commercial was over, she realized she was watching the local news station.

"State and federal agencies concluded a months-long trespass pot-farm investigation outside Alta early this morning with the arrests of close to 40 workers, drivers, and others employed by what is believed to be a Mexican drug cartel. Officials seized records, equipment, and goods at the site, which was being cleared for spring planting. Still at large is Felix Ortez, alleged to be one of the leaders of the operation.

Sheriff's deputies used canine DNA typing to connect him to an abandoned farm discovered earlier this month outside St. Cross. Anyone seeing a person they believe to be Ortez should call local law enforcement. He is considered armed and dangerous."

A dated mug shot of Ortez appeared behind the newscaster.

Harper studied the face but had no clue if he was the man at the shelter. That would explain why he remained at large, however. She jumped when the phone rang.

"Harper," Frank said. "How are you doing? Are you okay?"

"I'm in one piece," she said. "Slept most of the day away. How about you?"

"Been better," Frank said. "Think I'm getting a bit old for volunteer night work, however. You run a mean operation over there at that shelter, lady. Rousting folks at all hours. Have you seen the news?"

"Yes, I was just watching it," she said. "Wondering if Ortez was the one who caused the trouble at the shelter. I never got a good look at the guy."

"Well, I just got off the phone with Jessie. The tire track images taken from the pound match some taken from the trespass plantation," Frank said. "I'd say you had a close call last night."

Harper shuddered and closed her eyes. She remembered the intruder's low voice, almost like a growl.

"Another thing," Frank said. "That drug sweep at the church was a false alarm. Turns out the hand bell thief placed the call trying to cause more trouble. Sheriff's deputies were able to trace her rambling call, and she's been arrested."

"Why would someone do that?" Harper asked. "A vendetta against the church? Mental illness?"

"Beats me," Frank said. "Jessie is being pretty tight-lipped about the matter. Hey, you want me to bring you over some dinner?"

"I'd like nothing better," Harper said, "but I've got a date with your friend Hans." She immediately wished she had given him an excuse rather than the truth.

"Oh," Frank said, somewhat taken aback. "I didn't think he'd be your type."

"Excuse me?" she asked, on the defensive. "What's that mean?"

"He just has a reputation as a bit of a playboy."

"Then why did you have him show me around at the party?"

"Oh, he's a popular guy," Frank said. "I knew he'd get you introduced to everyone. I just don't want to see you get hurt."

"What?" Harper said. She was angry and it

showed. "I think I can take care of myself in that department, Frank."

"Just a friendly warning," Frank said, his voice cool. "Have a nice evening."

After she put the phone down, Harper thought again about Frank's controlling nature and his short temper. And what was that tone in Frank's voice? Disapproval that she accepted a date with Hans or regret that he hadn't asked first?

Harper took her time getting ready for the evening. Black jeans seemed to be what passed for dressy attire around these parts. She studied her shape in the full-length mirror. Perhaps working at the shelter was firming up her midsection.

While styling her hair with a blow dryer, the phone rang again. She didn't recognize the number on the display.

"Harper, this is Sammie. That drug lord guy on the news? He came into the shelter the night you asked me to close up for you. Friday night."

"You're kidding!" Harper said. "I mean, I know you're not. Sheesh. Did you tell the police?"

"No," Sammie said. "My folks would kill me. They'd think I was buying from him or something."

"Sammie, think this through. First of all, do you even smoke weed?"

There was silence on the other end of the

line. Finally Sammie spoke. "I've tried it but, no, not regularly or anything. It's just, if my parents think it's dangerous to work at the shelter, they won't let me continue."

"But isn't your 'sentence' about up anyway?" Harper asked.

"Well, yeah, but I was thinking I might stay on ... at least on Saturdays. It's not like there's so much else to do around this place."

Harper was caught off guard, but pleased, by Sammie's decision.

"I don't think there's any way around this, Sammie, since you're still a minor," Harper said. "Tell your folks you saw this guy, and they can notify the sheriff's office. Have them ask for Officer Grady. She's a good cop, and you can trust her. If there's a problem with your continuing at the shelter, I will talk to your parents."

They rang off.

25

Dinner with Hans turned out to be quite fun, once Harper got over the fact that he picked her up in a late model Ferrari. Who in St. Cross drove a Ferrari, even one speckled with rust spots?

"I like the yellow color," Harper said. She hopped in the passenger side. "Stunning."

"Harper, it's a Ferrari," Hans said with mock seriousness. "We call this color Giallo Modena, not yellow. It's very rare these days."

"Not quite what I expected," Harper said, as he put the sports car in gear.

"I tinker in trading tech stocks and restoring old cars – one hobby modestly fueling the other," he said. "No one ever got rich working as a fire-prevention officer."

"Why do you do it?" Harper asked.

Hans watched the road for a moment before he answered. "My work, you mean? I value community service, and I've a long, deep love-affair with nature. When I transferred in to St. Cross I felt like I was home. I couldn't imagine living anywhere else."

Before long, they were pulling into the parking lot at the Stock Exchange. As Harper had suspected, the vintage establishment specialized in steaks and beef dishes. The dark rough wood interiors played well against the white linen tablecloths. Candlelight added a touch of elegance.

After studying the menu, Harper splurged on a filet mignon for her entrée. Hans selected a bottle of California red wine. She was not disappointed in either.

Hans kept the conversation moving, recounting the history of every car he had ever owned. Although she'd had to stifle a yawn at one point – she wasn't used to drinking more than one glass of wine – overall Harper found Hans charming and very amusing. *Funny,* Harper thought, *if I'd have seen him across a room, I would have guessed he was the strong silent type.*

"So what about you, Harper? Are you finding your fit in St. Cross now that you're working at the animal shelter?"

"Not yet, but I supposed these things take

time. I'm like a fish out of water at the shelter still. I do, however, feel connected in the choir. Music has that kind of power – to bring people together despite their differences."

Hans' infectious smile made the collegial man a perfect dinner date. Harper was able to put the stresses of the past few weeks aside and relax. Since Hans towered over her when they were standing, and she'd been perched somewhat awkwardly on the couch arm at the party, the dinner was the first time she had really been able to get a good look at him. His long face was handsome. Delicate wrinkles branched out from the outer corners of his eyes, and he had deep laugh lines. She guessed he was near her age. *I just wish he wouldn't talk so much.*

In Hans' travels he had collected handicrafts and art from indigenous people.

"You must come to my house, and I will show you pottery and weaving from all the continents – well, at least two, anyway," he said. "Best of all, I have a hot tub. This is the American Dream, no?"

Harper laughed.

Next Hans was off on a tangent about water-pollution problems from the area's legacy of gold mining – a topic he was obviously passionate about.

"Early miners panned for gold by running sediment through sluice boxes and adding mercury to bind the gold," he said. "The mercury is still finding its way downstream and into the food supply. Do you have your own well, Harper?"

"Why, yes."

"You should get your water quality checked sometime this spring," he said. "One never knows. With the drought, the water tables are lower, and the mercury can be more concentrated."

"Really?" Harper said. "I didn't realize there were old mines so close to town."

"That's what made the land-owning Cross family so rich," he said. "Not the land they owned, but what was found on it. If only we could tap the remaining estate monies to help fund the mercury clean-up. But I shouldn't say that to you now that you have gone to the dark side."

"The dark side? What are you talking about?"

"Now that you work for the Cross family estate – at the shelter," Hans said. "Damage to the environment remains long after they are all gone. Yet their wealth continues to fund their pet projects – no pun intended. There's a lot of animosity about that in some circles."

"I didn't realize," Harper said and trailed off.

Eventually Hans slowed down, and Harper brought him up to speed on the Requiem performance and the events in the early morning hours. “You amaze me, Harper Henshaw,” Hans said. “First you rescue our Frankie, and now you’ve escaped a dangerous drug criminal. You are a powerhouse packed into a subcompact.” She shook her head at his corniness. *Is this guy for real,* she wondered.

After dinner, Hans and Harper went to the local watering hole for a nightcap.

“English is a mystery,” Hans said, “how the same word for an after-dinner drink is a hat for sleeping.”

The saloon had a heavy wooden bar and table seating in the front, and a pool table in the back. Once Harper decided on an Irish cream, Hans placed their orders with the bartender. They selected a table near the door. Harper would not normally go inside a bar, and would never have gone unaccompanied, so she soaked up the atmosphere and enjoyed people-watching. A waitress brought their drinks, and Hans paid. As usual, he seemed to know a lot of the locals.

“Who are these people?” Harper asked.

“Many are Forest Service workers, such as that table of two men and two women over there,” he said discreetly pointing. “You might recognize them from the cleanup. We’ll have another one planned soon, now that the site outside Alta has been discovered.

“A few others are local merchants or people I’ve seen around town. Some are Edison workers who come up from the power plant partway down the mountain. I don't recognize the four men at the pool table. They are probably flatlanders."

"Flatlanders?" Harper asked. "Meaning tourists? I thought St. Cross was off the tourist beat."

"A few find us from time to time," Hans said. "They aren't necessarily tourists, just people who live in the valley. If this was fall, this place would be full of hunters – and trimmers come into town for some fun."

"Trimmers?" Harper asked.

"Yeah. Young people who travel to chase jobs harvesting pot," Hans said. "They pull the plants and cut off all the excess leaves to prep the pot for sale. There's good money in it. They are also known as trimmigrants."

"Meaning they are foreign born? Mexicans?"

"Not necessarily. A lot are hippies and college students. That's also why you'll see a few more women in here in the fall. Trimming requires nimble fingers and dexterity. Some of the best trimmers are women."

"That must really improve the dating pool."

"Not for me," Hans said. "Those women are fools to work on the illegal plantations. There are stories of assaults and rape – some of the trimmers turn to prostitution. Beyond the damage to the environment, illegal pot plantations are an ugly industry."

As Hans continued, Harper was amazed at how ignorant she had been about mountain life.

"Looks like this group of flatlanders may be hogging the pool table. See the quarters lined up along the side? Those are from people waiting to play. But out-of-towners sometimes think if they have a big stack of quarters they can continue to play until they are used up. Local rules say otherwise.

"Uh-oh. See that mountain-sized man with the bun who just rose? I think he plans to educate them a little."

Harper watched entranced as the large man ambled over to the table. Words soon turned into shouts and escalated into a shoving match.

"Harper, finish your drink," Hans said. "Let's get out of here before a full-blown brawl breaks out."

When Hans returned Harper to her doorstep, things got a little awkward – first date awkward. *What is dating protocol these days,* Harper wondered. She decided to err on the part of caution and say her goodbye on the porch.

"Thank you, Hans," she said. "The evening was a great distraction, but I am exhausted and expected at the shelter tomorrow."

Hans squatted to get a good look at her face.

"Harper, I know I am something of a Nordic giant and you are a Lilliputian," he said, "but I do hope you will do me the honor of a second date. I think this was not so horrible."

She couldn't help but laugh.

"I'll see you Friday, when I do your site check, and we can talk about it then," Hans said. Then he bent over, gave her a soft kiss on the cheek and whispered in her ear. "Harper I do not think I can kiss you well if we are standing."

"Next time," she said, her voice husky.

Hans was speeding by the Simpsons' house at the same time P.W. happened to be looking out into the inky black sky. Even in the dark, P.W. could make out the distinctive yellow sports car.

Wonder what Hans has been up to tonight, he mused.

Sleep was eluding the old man, so he decided to make the most of the spare time. He headed to the hall closet.

Aza had outgrown more than half of his winter outerwear. *No time like the present for a little spring cleaning,* P.W. thought, flicking on the hall light. *Closing that closet has become like trying to fit 10 pounds of ....* He didn't finish the saying.

P.W. wandered into the kitchen to grab a large garbage bag.

Back in the hall he yanked out two snow suits, a jacket, and a vest that he knew were too small for Aza. Then he tried to match up all the gloves and mittens. A small pair went directly into the bag along with a couple of knit caps. He'd take the items to the thrift store in case anyone could use them. He checked the pockets of the snow suits, fishing out an assortment of rocks and candy wrappers. Next he inspected the jacket. A feather and some chewing gum were among the treasures there.

When he put his hand into the vest pocket, however, he felt a familiar shape. There was his missing chain with the house and old church keys on it. He had always thought the boy had misplaced those keys. *Well, I'll be.*

Once the closet was in order, P.W. killed the lights and sat in his favorite chair. He looked out into the night. His thoughts were far away from the present – about 20 years, in fact. The visit to his old stomping grounds had set him thinking. He recalled the night Edith Saint Cross drew her last breath. The hard-headed woman had insisted on staying in her own home, even though her heart was failing. Perhaps if he had insisted she go to the hospital, Edith wouldn't have died that night. But she was never one to be bullied into doing anything.

Edith had asked him to put on a recording of Pachelbel's Canon. They listened and then chatted late into the evening. He could recall scraps of the conversation they had about church business that night. "You must have seen a lot of changes in the church during your lifetime," P.W. had said at one point. Ever stubborn, Edith had said: "Yes, and I've resisted every one of them." P.W. had fallen asleep in the armchair that sat in her bedroom. When he awoke the next morning, she was dead. How many times had he relived that evening in his mind? He couldn't even begin to count. All he knew was that he missed his old friend and felt it wouldn't be long before he followed her.

26

The next day at the pound provided a welcome return to normality for Harper. There were routines to be followed. Frank had set up procedures that allowed little margin for error.

The animals needed to be fed and watered. Kennels needed to be cleaned out. Dogs needed to be walked. Then, in whatever time was left after helping visitors, there was the eternal chore of grooming. Most of the animals that wound up at the pound needed a good bath. And, of course, everything required paperwork.

"How is it," Harper asked Vi, "that staff and volunteers can seem to do nothing wrong for the dogs, who appreciate any attention they receive? The cats, however, have ideas of their own."

"Not everyone understands felines," Vi said in her matter-of-fact way. She came in weekday mornings and stayed through mid-afternoon. Privately, Harper had begun to think of the efficient woman as the cat whisperer. She was relieved that Vi took charge of most of the cat duties.

Sammie was expected after school if any animals needed bathing. Harper crossed her fingers that Sammie's folks would allow the teenager to return.

Buck would show up around the time Harper was calling it a day. She found the predictable schedule comforting.

Desk traffic was light by early afternoon, so Harper stepped outside for a quick break. The sky was blue with puffy white clouds that scudded along on the breeze. Many of the dogs were in their chain-link-enclosed runs, enjoying the sunlight.

She walked to the back and reentered the kennel area to work on laundering the dog bedding that had been swapped out after yesterday's fiasco. A mountain of blankets and comforters spilled from the utility room, where two industrial washers and dryers stood.

Once the laundry was in motion, she stopped by Delilah's kennel and poked a finger through the wire. "You're winning the lottery today, little lady," she said. "I think we'll get along just fine."

She was stroking the corgi's muzzle with one finger when Vi found her. "PD called.

Bringing in two dogs, one deceased. I'll notify the vet's office to pick up the carcass. ETA 10 minutes."

Harper finished up her chores and went out the back door to assist with the new arrival. Two black-and-whites pulled up. She was surprised to see Jessie emerge from one of them. After yesterday's big drug bust, she thought that perhaps the deputy would have a day off.

She started toward Jessie's vehicle but was waved off. "I've got the deceased canine. Take care of the other first."

Harper's second surprise was that she recognized the dog. The bull terrier that had been taken from the shelter during the night – one of the evidence dogs – was in the back seat of the other cruiser. After she kenneled it, she grabbed a couple of extra-large heavy duty trash bags, a stretcher and met Jessie at the trunk of her car.

There she found the dead Presa Canario, its gigantic head covered in dried blood.

"What happened?" Harper asked.

"Far as we can tell, the guy who took the dogs?" Jessie said. "His truck went off the road and down an embankment. He appears to have been killed by the impact. Based on the preliminary ID, it looks like we caught up with Felix Ortez."

After the officers left, Harper found Vi finishing up the paperwork on the intake dog.

"I can do that, Vi," Harper said. "You've stayed past the end of your shift."

"Don't pay it no mind," she said. "I'm almost done, and then I'm outta here. You go back to the front."

Vi made sure that the kennel was clearly tagged with the proper paperwork attached in a plastic pouch. The one thing that remained was to give the dog a name.

She grabbed the black permanent marker. A hint of a grin pulled at her mouth. Carefully, she filled in the blank line for the dog's name.

Harper left through the back door that evening. She stopped at the corgi's kennel to leash her up. "Come on, Delilah," she said. "You're going home."

As she headed out, the red kennel tag caught her eye. Vi had given the evidence dog the name of Samson. "Oh, brother," Harper said. She shut the door behind herself.

27

The days at the pound passed quickly for Harper. She enjoyed the camaraderie of the small dedicated staff and regular volunteers. Being around people on a daily basis suited her somewhat introverted personality. She didn't necessarily need to interact with them, but she liked being part of a team as much as she had at the newspaper. Getting used to the stench of the shelter was another matter. Summer heat, no doubt, would bring the odor up another notch.

Harper was sitting at the front desk in the reception area when her cell phone buzzed. The display read: G DONOFRIO.

"Hey, there," Harper said. "Don't tell me you need me to bail you out again?"

"Funny," Gene said. "Your story on the Cross homestead did really well by the way. The online readers have been loving it. And thanks for sending the old photos that Simpson supplied. Exclusive material never hurts."

"So, what's up?" Harper asked.

"Well, strange as it may seem, perhaps that was a fire-sale price on the old Cross estate. Place just went into escrow. And the buyer looks to be a pretty interesting guy: A millionaire who probably doesn't need another piece of real estate. My guess is he'll use it as a second or third home. Must have wanted a spot in the mountains, but it beats me why he would buy in such a remote area. You're not exactly airport-close there."

"Interesting," Harper said. "Let me guess. You want me to do a follow-up story."

Gene grunted. "What a sleuth! We'll see how the deal plays out first. If the mansion closes, then I'll offer you first right of refusal. We're just going to run a brief on the pending sale. Thought I'd let you know, though. Hopefully we can get the seller to talk to us for the larger piece."

"Hey, Gene. Did you have a chance to look at the pot farm cleanup story?"

"Yeah, that's a winner, Harper. I've just been waiting for my budget to balance before we publish it. The red ink here is killing me."

"I understand. Let me know when you plan to run the piece."

Harper had just gotten off the phone when

Vi appeared and dropped a stack of applications on the desk.

"What's this?"

"Applications for summer work," Vi said. "They've been coming in since you started, and I've been collecting them while you felt your way around. But time's a-wasting. We'll need to staff up for the busy summer months. Between employee vacations and the second-home people showing up and doubling the population, this place gets crazy. You've just been enjoying the down time."

"Oh, great. Thanks."

Harper leafed through the stack and was about to set it aside to read later when she spied a familiar name. Samantha Hernandez was among the applicants looking for paid summer employment. Most of the others were college students who went to Sierra Foothills. Further down in the pile she found one from Jim Becker, filled out with his college address. *Interesting,* she thought. She'd take the applications home and pore over them in the company of her dog. At least she had two candidates whom she already knew and liked.

As Harper became more familiar with the kennel procedures and routine, the operation felt less foreign to her. One thing that bothered her, though, was the evidence dog. What kind of life was it for an animal to be stuck in a kennel or the yard before being shipped to County for possible euthanasia? So, remembering what Hans had said – that she worked for the Cross estate – Harper had started taking the dog on daily walks, even though it was against the shelter's written policy.

Wouldn't Edith have wanted that – to give the dog the best possible life while it was in her care? The staff members who knew this was a departure from the rules turned a blind eye. The volunteers didn't question her. She was the boss, after all.

The main phone at the shelter, which had been quiet most of the afternoon, rang. Harper grabbed it on the second ring.

"St. Cross Animal Shelter. This is Harper Henshaw. How may I assist you?"

The caller had found a beagle in his barn that had given birth to pups. Several were dead. The mother was weak and thirsty. She had downed two bowls of water and eaten some lunch meat the homeowner had provided. Harper took down the address. "Someone will be right out."

One thing Harper was learning on the job was not to bother Animal Control if she could help it. They were usually hours, if not days, away, depending on how backed up they were, and her staff could handle most small-animal situations. She buzzed the back and got Buck.

"I think our missing beagle has turned up. There's a mother and some pups out at the Jacob place on Route 91. You want to grab a dog carrier and head on out there?

"Caller says some of the pups appear to be dead. Just take them straight to the vet's to be checked out. I think our credit's still good. Thanks."

All in a day's work, Harper thought.

28

P.W. had been meaning to call Frank for a while. Then events had piled one upon the other. The dang fool had stepped in that animal trap, then there was the pot plantation cleanup with all that entailed at the church site, and then the performance of the Requiem. That concert had almost been too much for P.W. He was going to retire from choir – although he might lend his deep bass voice for the occasional funeral.

Aza, of course, seemed to take up every extra minute of P.W.'s time with schoolwork, meal preparation, and a never-ending pile of dirty laundry. The days had sped by before P.W. realized it. Not having to be on the church site as frequently, however, meant his time was opening up a little. He placed the call before the idea fell out of his mind again. He had waited long enough.

"Frank," P.W. said, absentmindedly stroking the top of Sheldon's head. "We need to talk. Come on by sometime today while Aza is in school."

"Sure thing," Frank said. "Why don't I bring us up some takeout lunch from the Klatch? See you about noon."

P.W. finished the breakfast dishes and then settled into his favorite chair with a mug of hot coffee for what he called his "long morning think." Frank's rap on the front door awakened him hours later.

"Hey, sleeping beauty," Frank said to P.W. as he let himself in through the unlocked front door. "Rise and shine."

"Just resting my eyes," P.W. said. "They've seen too much for one lifetime."

Frank left the food on the drop-leaf dining table and went in search of plates and silverware. P.W. took his time unfolding from the easy chair and getting to the table.

"What did you do that for, Frank?" P.W. asked as he took his seat. He gestured to the plates. "I ain't too good to eat outta plastic."

"I'll wash," Frank said. "As I recall, Big W, you're the boss."

"Well, now, that's just the thing," P.W. said reaching inside his cardigan and pulling a long white envelope from his shirt pocket. "Maybe I am or maybe I ain't." He set the envelope, which had yellowed over the years, on the table between them.

He drew a deep breath before he spoke. "You never asked me why I had you pick up Aza that Saturday and was gone all day."

"Figured it was none of my business," Frank said. "But somehow I think you're going to tell me."

"Yep," P.W. said as he made inroads into his

food. After several minutes of chewing, he continued. "Had a routine checkup, but also I went to see Patricia Grayson to let her know my plan. Now, here's the thing."

Frank continued working on his turkey sandwich.

"You ever hear of a poison pill?"

"Sure," Frank said. "I was in finance years ago. Something that makes it harder for someone to take over a company. What's that got to do with anything?"

"Well, from the get-go Edith set something up as a kind of safety precaution to make sure her wishes were carried out – in case things got to going horribly wrong at some point." P.W. slid the envelope over to Frank. "And now it's yours."

Frank was confused. "What the – "

P.W. raised his hand to silence the younger man.

"Ms. Grayson, of course, has known about this all along. Those last weeks, when Edith was dying, they set the whole thing up, layer upon layer, some parts with me at her bedside, and other times with just the lawyers when I wasn't there. We would laugh about it as she came up with each cockamamie detail. But she was dead serious about her money being used for good works.

"Remember when I became church caretaker

10 years ago? Well, this letter came with the job," P.W. said. "Edith called it the key. Just as the caretaker gets the keys to the church, he or she also is the keeper of the key. I swear, Edith watched too many dramas near the end. Just go ahead and read it."

Frank gingerly opened the envelope. He was expecting a typed correspondence from the law office, like the ones he had seen in the past, but inside was a letter penned in Edith's own spidery handwriting. The faded document was dated a week before her death and witnessed by her attorney. Frank skimmed the letter from start to finish and then reread it more carefully a second time. He let out a low whistle.

> Dearest Phinehas,
>
> If all has gone according to plan, you are reading this at the 10th anniversary of my death. The lawyers have kept things operating smoothly, but the time has come to reveal my hand.
>
> I can think of no one else I trust more to see my estate's work into the future. For as long as the money holds out, someone needs to function as the overseer of the estate – the ultimate arbitrator when snares and snags crop up. Your wishes will be incorporated into the periodic codicils, so you will be

> controlling the operation of the estate going forward.
>
> This letter grants you that authority until you die or pass it on to another soul whom you trust. I know this responsibility will be a burden, so I thank you in advance.
>
> As for your successor, choose carefully. I can't know when you will pass this on and who will be in your inner circle then.
>
> I can't repay you in this lifetime, so I'll be getting things ready for you on the other side of the great divide. I'm sure you will have missed my company greatly by the time you decide to join me.
>
> With sincerest gratitude,
> Edith

Frank sat silently, letting the information register.

P.W. resumed talking. "She couldn't know what the future would hold. What if the church was no longer viable? What if the county put in its own animal shelter in town, and ours became unnecessary? So she set it up that, a decade after her death, I became the keeper of the key, so to speak. I can close down either of those places at any time and convert them to another use ... as long as it serves the public good."

Frank shook his head from side to side in bewilderment. "But why did she select me to head the animal shelter? Or for anything? I could never figure that out. I knew who she was, but we weren't in the same circles. I maybe spoke to her a coupla times at church."

"Ah, you see, that's the thing," P.W. said. "She didn't pick you. I did."

Frank was speechless.

"Think about it," P.W. said. "She had to have someone she could trust, and that was me. And I have to have someone I can trust, so I'm picking you. When you are done being the keeper, you'll pick the next one."

Frank sputtered. "But the codicils, the pound job .... She chose me for that."

"Nope," P.W. said. "I did.

"Frank, you were moping along with your life all those years after Teresa died. You needed a new direction. Someone needed to set you on a better path. I just took advantage of the situation. What better position for you to keep an eye on things at the church now, than as caretaker?

"You only thought you were in charge as chairman of the board. Never been one to gossip, but Lordy, the things I've seen."

P.W. didn't elaborate, and Frank didn't push for details. P.W. would give him more information when and if he was good and ready.

"Whoa," Frank said, trying to get his head

around all this new information. "What about Harper? How did she fit into the equation?"

"I picked her, of course," P.W. said. "Met her at choir the first night she came out for the Requiem and thought she was good people. Just maybe a little lost settling in here.

"Plus, I know you, Frank. You'd overlook her even if she was in your face. You are always looking for the 'perfect' woman. I'm not sure she exists anywhere except in your head. Now Harper, there's a real nice gal."

"Why, you old romantic fool," Frank said. "No wonder I kept getting the vibe that you were trying to set me up with her. But even you can't control that, my man. She's already dating Hans."

P.W. gave Frank the over-the-reading glasses stare he usually reserved for Aza. "Frank, you may be slightly over the hill, but I've never known a little competition to stand in your way of anything."

29

The new day started like so many others in that part of paradise. The morning mist was burning off in the canyons and valleys, and the sun was already heating up the granite faces of the Sierra Nevada Mountains.

Fine time for a hike, Frank thought. He picked up his cell phone and called Harper.

"Yes, I'd love to hike to the falls," Harper said. "I'll be over right after breakfast."

Delilah was too old for the strenuous hike Frank proposed, as were his dogs Grin and Barrett. Harper brought along Samson.

He was technically the county's dog. But since they wouldn't be calling for him on a weekend, Harper had started taking him home on Friday nights. Weekdays he could often be found sitting at her feet in the front office at the shelter.

Frank, to his credit, had not commented on the arrangement. He had his hands full at the church. Harper was in charge at the shelter.

Before long, the three of them were heading along the parkland trail behind Frank's house, and rising steadily through the ponderosa and Jeffrey pine canopy. The winter snows were melting at higher elevations, and icy water filled the rocky streambeds. The gushing cascade would be especially showy in the early light. Mountain chickadees filled the forest with sound, interrupted only by the hikers' footfalls and intermittent conversation.

"I never asked how your date with Hans went," Frank said as they walked abreast up the lower, wide portion of the earth-and-stone trail. He had a slight limp. A ground squirrel cut across ahead of them.

Harper shot him a sideways glance to read his countenance. He didn't appear to hold any resentment.

"The evening was great fun," she said, "although he is a bit hung up on cars. After a lovely dinner he took me to some dive bar until a fight broke out."

Frank laughed. "Don't worry. He has other hobbies. Come late fall I wouldn't be surprised if he tries to sign you up for the St. Cross Nordic skiing team."

"What's this?" Harper asked. "We have a ski

team?" Harper realized she had said "we" instead of "St. Cross."

"Not really a team so much as a social club," Frank said. "Hans sets up a bunch of trails, and club members meet on Saturday mornings to ski together. Maybe have a fun race. Then they spend the afternoon at the bar, drinking beer. Have you ever tried cross-country skiing?"

"No, but I have downhill skied. Cross-country sounds fun."

Soon the trail grew rockier and narrowed. Pines lined the path, and tree roots made for some unsteady footing. Frank dropped back to let Harper take the lead.

Frank studied Harper's form as he followed her up the mountain. He took in her ample hips; the shape of her calves, pale from a winter in long pants; how straight her waist was, viewed from behind. Absentmindedly, he rubbed the finger where his gold wedding band had been before he finally took it off years earlier. A smile creased his face. He felt so grateful – for his life, for his friends, for his good fortune to be able live in such natural beauty.

The sound of distant water interrupted his thoughts. They'd be at the base of the falls soon.

Suddenly he felt a panic rise from the depths of his being. Up ahead, Harper was rounding a rock outcropping. Frank rushed to Harper, twirled her towards him and grabbed her in an embrace, sheltering her head with one hand.

Harper stood motionless. “What?” she asked, eyes wide.

He took in a deep breath of her hair and released her.

“I’d just like to walk ahead for a while,” he said, “if you don’t mind.”

She looked into his serious eyes. Would she ever understand this man?

“By all means.”

Frank assumed the lead as Harper trailed. He seemed to be taking longer and longer strides as the waterfall neared, and she fell back, instinctively giving him more space. When she caught up with him, he was sitting on a stone shelf that had a tremendous view of the roaring falls. Clear cold water from melting snowpack cascaded over the granite, pulled by gravity into a pool below. Harper was astounded by how close they were to the falls and how the water tumbled down the mountainside.

But Frank wasn’t looking at the waterfall. His head was buried in his hands.

Harper sat down next to him and put her hand on his back. “Frank,” she said softly. “Are you okay?”

He shook his head from side to side. They sat listening to the sound of the water. Eventually he spoke.

“No, I’m not,” he said unsteadily. “Ghost from the past seems to have caught up with me.”

He wiped at his eyes with the back of his hand and buried his head again. Harper scooted up behind him and wrapped her arms around him from the back, straddling him with her legs. She rested her head on his spine and held him tightly as they gently rocked. They stayed that way until Frank’s storm had blown over. Then, without a word, they headed back down the mountain.

Coming Soon

Want to read more about the residents of St. Cross? Look for Redemption, *the next in the St. Cross Choir series.*

There weren't a lot of places for a proper date in St. Cross. The Northern California town's small population had the services of a church, an animal shelter, a general store, and three restaurants. The beef-centric Stock Exchange was the only upscale eatery. The Coffee Klatch, the local greasy spoon, was pretty public for a date. The Hole in the Wall, a dive bar, was too informal.

So, Frank O'Brien had opted for an Italian restaurant in the hub of Alta, some 20 miles away. The location and choice of a Thursday night meant that he and his date, fellow choir member Harper Henshaw, were likely to be away from the prying eyes of the St. Cross townsfolk. A romance, should their friendship come to that, would be hard to keep from the local gossips for long.

"It's been a while since I had good Italian food," Harper said. The dining room was more than half full, and the bar portion of the restaurant, packed. "What do you recommend, Frank?"

The weathered outdoorsman and the short fair-skinned redhead had been thrown together by circumstances soon after she moved to his tiny hometown of St. Cross in the Sierra Nevada Mountains. Hesitant to ask her out after a string of failed romances, the longtime widower could no longer ignore his feelings. He liked the spunky newcomer and finally felt he was willing to see where their relationship might lead.

"You can't go wrong here." Frank wasn't one to leave much to chance. "Personally I'm a sucker for the chicken parmesan, and they really know their way around a roasted vegetable. The Brussels sprouts are a great starter. Shall I pick a wine? They have some great reds, if that works with what you'll be ordering."

"Sure thing," Harper said. "Pick away." As the waiter came and took their wine order, she studied the décor. The tasteful contemporary interiors were somewhat oddly paired with framed historical photographs. Since moving to the Sierra Nevada mountain community she had been inside many a dated building. Most of the development in this part of the range appeared to have come in waves during the 1920s, the 1950s, and the 1990s. No doubt the old-time black-and-white photos were from the '20s, when the area was booming with prospectors.

The waiter returned bearing a familiar Cabernet Sauvignon from a Paso Robles winery. Harper had brought the same label to Frank's house when he had hosted a small dinner party shortly after her move to the mountains.

"Frank, I can't believe you remembered."

"Good wine, great company, what's not to love? Let's say we toast to that."

For Harper's part, she had been attracted to Frank from the first time they met. Oh, she knew the sometimes mercurial and controlling man wasn't perfect, and that her initial response had been a physical one, but she too was ready to see where their friendship might be headed.

Harper was savoring her first sip of the wine when Frank abruptly set down his glass. He was staring intently over her shoulder, his rugged face a mixture of disbelief and anger. He pushed his chair back to rise.

"Harper, call 911."

"What?" she said, but Frank was already on his feet and moving like a locomotive to the bar. He snatched a drink off the counter and handed it to the bartender. "Keep that for evidence," he said. Then he confronted the man next to the empty spot where the cocktail had sat.

"I saw you put something into your

companion's drink when she left for the restroom," Frank said.

"Bullshit," said the gaunt-looking man, who rose and towered over Frank. By then Harper was on the line with 911, but not really sure what she was reporting. A soon-to-be brawl? The bartender tried to defuse the situation.

"Chill," he said. "I'm sure there's a logical explanation for this. Billy here is a regular. I can vouch for him. You flatlanders can't come in here and cause a ruckus." The restaurant manager joined the fray.

"I am not a flatlander," Frank said. He practically hissed the derogatory term for those from the Central Valley. Frank addressed the manager. "I saw your patron drop something into his date's drink. Police are on their way."

The manager looked skeptical. "I'm Ray Tunney. We run a fine dining establishment here. There's obviously been some sort of misunderstanding. Barkeep, make Billy's date a new drink."

With a swift movement the bartender splashed the contents of the drink in question into the sink. Frank couldn't believe his eyes. He reached over to wrestle the glass away just as the bartender started to rinse it out. "There are penalties for destroying evidence."

Harper, who had been watching the action with her phone to her ear, was on her feet and into the ladies room seconds later. There she told the only woman in the restroom what was going on outside. By the time the two women emerged, a sheriff's deputy was on the scene.

The young cop was someone Frank knew. Russ Wilson had started his days as a rookie in the territory that included St. Cross. Frank, in his capacity as church caretaker, had met Russ on several occasions. Recently, however, Russ had been covering a beat in Alta. As the deputy attempted to sort out the chain of events, his backup arrived. Soon the two uniforms were taking statements from the bartender and the manager. Russ bagged the empty glass as evidence.

Frank gave his name to the other deputy. The bartender, within ear shot, let out a low whistle.

"Frank O'Brien? I remember that name. Isn't he the wife basher from over in St. Cross?"

Harper, who had returned to their table, watched from what had been his seat as Frank fought to maintain his control. She knew that Frank had lost his late wife in a hiking accident, but he had never mentioned that there had been any suspicions of foul play. Harper mentally scolded herself for not researching the incident before accepting the date. She had once been an investigative journalist. Why hadn't her reporter's instincts kicked in earlier?

When the deputies left, the manager made it clear to Frank and Harper that they were no longer welcome to stay for dinner. The disruption had cost the restaurant a fair chunk of the evening's trade.

So the pair headed back to St. Cross in Frank's late-model truck. He was as agitated as Harper had ever seen him. She let him fume a long time before she brought up the incident.

"What do you think that was about, Frank?" she asked tentatively.

"Hell if I know," Frank said. "Looked to me like a textbook case of a guy dropping a roofie in a date's drink."

"A roofie?" Harper asked.

"Yeah, it's a date rape drug – rophynol – a tranquilizer about 10 times as powerful as Valium. Unfortunately, it's not uncommon among a segment of college students. Probably be easy to get in Alta."

Harper thought of the students she knew from the local Sierra Foothills College. She couldn't imagine any of them using a date rape drug. But she also didn't imagine that the singers and musicians she was thinking of were the part of the student population to which Frank was referring.

"I can't believe the bartender threw the drink away and rinsed the glass. Do you think the police will be able to find any traces of the drug?"

Frank sighed. "Unlikely. You can also test for the drug in urine but he popped it in the glass when she got up and she never had a drop of the drink. What's unbelievable to me is how the bartender and even the manager closed ranks. I started to feel like I was the criminal.

"I'm sorry, Harper. I'm not up for finishing this date tonight. I'm gonna drop you at your place and call it an evening. Will you take a raincheck?"

"Certainly."

Harper could see Frank was bothered by how the roofie incident ended. She liked that about him. Behind his in-control exterior, he had a depth of emotion that she found intriguing. But the "wife basher" comment would need to be addressed if their relationship was ever going anywhere.

After driving the rest of the way in silence, Frank pulled into Harper's pine tree-lined driveway and killed the ignition outside her front porch.

She kept her eyes straight ahead and posed the question. "I have to ask. Why did the bartender recognize your name and mention your late wife?"

Frank worked to regulate his breathing. Then gave her a reply she did not want to hear.

"Get out," he said, "please."

CPSIA information can be obtained
at www.ICGtesting.com
Printed in the USA
FSOW01n1931301017
40536FS

9 781478 785293